AUDRA NORTH

Midlife Crisis

RIPTIDE
PUBLISHING

Riptide Publishing
PO Box 1537
Burnsville, NC 28714
www.riptidepublishing.com

Midlife Crisis
Copyright © 2017 by Audra North

Cover art: L.C. Chase, lcchase.com/design.htm
Editor: Sarah Lyons
Layout: L.C. Chase, lcchase.com/design.htm

ISBN: 978-1-62649-668-2

First edition
August, 2017

Also available in ebook:
ISBN: 978-1-62649-645-3

AUDRA NORTH

Midlife Crisis

RIPTIDE
PUBLISHING

For A.B.

TABLE OF
Contents

Chapter One

At the front end of the bar, Cam McGhee sat huddled over a bottle of Shiner, trying to ignore his discomfort.

Perhaps some part of his subconscious was *trying* to make sure everyone else in here knew he didn't belong. Maybe that was why he'd chosen to sit in the one place that meant braving the blast of chilly air that blew in every time someone walked through the front door. Or why he was scratching at the corner of the label of his beer bottle instead of sipping highballs like the other men in the bar.

Then again, he hadn't worked up the nerve to take his eyes off the longneck to check if anyone was so much as looking in his general direction, so how would he know for sure?

As it was, Cam's behavior on this—his first time in a gay bar—was remarkably similar to how he acted at Rex's place back home. Nothing remarkable, much less worth even a passing glance.

Which was why it surprised him when a slender blond in a pair of tight rocker jeans and a sheer white T-shirt sidled up to him on the neighboring stool.

"Hey there." The stranger's voice was neither high nor low—unlike Cam's gravelly baritone—and, at first, Cam thought he was a kid. The guy was dressed like he wasn't more than Elijah's age, anyway. But when Cam turned his head to look more closely, the overhead lighting flickered for a moment over a web of fine lines around blue eyes, a slight droop along the blond's jawline. Cam guessed the man was in his midthirties. Still twenty years younger than Cam, but not knee-jerk-recoil young.

"Hi," Cam managed to reply, lifting his bottle and tipping it slightly toward his new neighbor. The corner of the label curled down, the paper half-pulled from the glass, which made him frown. Next to this slick-haired, sparkling man-boy, the ravaged label looked out of place. Hell, he looked out of place. He'd known that already, but for the first time since he'd walked in, it dawned on him that he stood out much more than he'd initially believed. No one else was wearing anything even remotely similar to navy-blue Dickies and a long-sleeved chambray button-down. There were a few other African-American men, several others with graying hair, but despite his ability to find those similarities in the crowd, he knew he didn't blend in.

The people here all looked so . . . *city*.

"I'm Alex," the blond said, leaning slightly toward Cam for a moment before drawing back. A not-quite shoulder bump.

Was that supposed to be in lieu of a handshake? Cam wasn't sure. Everything felt impossibly foreign to him.

"Cam." *His* shoulders didn't budge.

But Alex didn't seem to notice, or maybe he simply didn't care, since he grinned and followed up with a sly look and slight smoothing of his voice when he asked, "Are you new in town? I've never seen you in here before."

Cam nodded. "Been here a week."

Alex laughed, which confused Cam, because he didn't think he'd said anything particularly funny. Maybe this was flirting. What would he know about it, anyway? He'd never really flirted with anyone. Not even his wife.

"I like your accent. Where you from?" Alex looked at Cam curiously over the rim of his glass as he took a sip. Alex had slim wrists. Slim, but still masculine, the sharp bones and stark veins covered with fine gold hairs that meandered up the back of his hand. The sleek, edgy look hadn't been doing much for Cam, but those wrists sure did.

He made a small sound and shrugged. "Nowhere near here." Last week he'd made the five-hour drive from Bitter, a rural, predominantly black farming town of six thousand people, to this crowded, bustling city, the bed of his truck packed with two serviceable suitcases and an assortment of power tools.

But he didn't feel like sharing that. Bitter was too small a place to go telling everyone in the wider world that he was from there.

"Texas, though, right?" Alex didn't seem to mind Cam's reticence, and Cam found himself increasingly grateful that someone else was dogged determined enough to carry this one through. Maybe he'd get what he came for tonight, after all.

Cam nodded.

"I always had a thing for country boys," Alex told him, and Cam nearly choked on the swig of beer he was taking. Alex grinned as though he knew he was saying disconcerting things—and liked it. "What brings you to Austin?"

Cam plunked the bottle back down on the bar. "Taking a vacation." He thought about stopping his reply, but figured he'd been taciturn enough already. He didn't want to drive Alex away. It wasn't likely to get much easier than this. "I'm here for a few months, taking a sabbatical of sorts."

Alex's eyebrows went up. "Are you a professor or something?"

Cam laughed at that. *Hardly.* "Nah. Just been working too hard for too long. I needed a break." That was true, though not really the reason for getting away from Bitter. "What do you do?"

"I'm in finance." Alex sat up straighter, and Cam assumed this meant that his job was something to be proud of. "I do investments, a lot of private portfolios, that kind of thing."

"Sounds interesting."

Alex nodded. "It is. The first ten years were intense but lucrative. Now it's just as exciting, but I don't have to bust my ass eighty hours a week anymore. That's for the junior-level schmucks." His chuckle was nasty and off-putting, but there was something oddly sexy about the way his hair glinted in the bar lights. He was a pretty, if slightly tarnished, white boy.

Cam decided to focus on that.

"So, what are you here for tonight, Cam?" Alex was fingering the rim of his glass and looking up at Cam through his lashes. *Pretty.*

Arousal hit hard, nearly making Cam grunt with the unexpected force of it. "Something different, I guess. Exploring."

"I'm up for something different too," Alex purred. Even in the low light, it was impossible to mistake the greedy hunger in his eyes in response to Cam's words, and Cam immediately wished he could take them back. Alex wasn't his type; he already knew that without going any further. But it had already taken so much to come this far tonight, and he had a goal.

He wanted his first kiss with another man to be over and done with.

Speaking of . . . Alex was already leaning forward, his lips coming together, coming *toward* Cam's.

Cam jerked back with a slight shake of his head. "Not here."

Over and done with didn't mean *public*.

Alex grinned. "You want to go somewhere more private?"

Yes. No. I don't know. He steeled himself against the surge of doubt that threatened to knock him over. "Yeah. Let's go."

His stomach clenched, feeling unnaturally full of nothing. He took one last swig of his beer, trying to stuff the discomfort out of himself, pushed cash toward the bartender, and followed Alex toward the exit.

Outside the bar, it was shockingly quiet. Alex turned to Cam, slid a hand up his arm, and squeezed the muscle with a murmur of appreciation. "My place?"

Cam nodded, unable to find his voice.

Alex didn't miss a beat, though. "I live just a couple blocks over." He pointed downtown toward Second Street. "Are you parked nearby? You can bring your car to my garage if you want."

Cam shook his head. "I'm in the lot over on Eighth. It's not much farther. No need to drive over." He blinked. Given the confusion knocking his brain around, it was strange to find that words were actually coming out of his mouth in some reasonable facsimile of conversation.

One more arm squeeze and Alex jerked his head toward the direction he'd pointed earlier and started walking. The clip-clop of their shoes was the only sound between them as they covered the block.

"Do you always wear cowboy boots?" Walking side by side in the streetlamp-lit low light, Cam couldn't see Alex's face, but it sounded like he was laughing, and Cam found himself smiling back. The weird cramp in his gut was slowly dissipating as he walked, and by the time they reached the crosswalk, he was feeling more in control.

He told himself that going home with Alex was a *good* thing. It was a good plan. They'd . . . well, they'd probably do a bit more than kissing, but that was okay. Being able to say he'd done it would go a long way toward settling the deeper unrest he'd been experiencing since LaVerne passed.

The *WALK* sign lit up. "I only wear them on Sundays and when I go out somewhere nice," he admitted as they crossed the street. "Most of the time it's steel-toed Carhartts."

On the opposite corner, Alex stopped and turned to stare at Cam. "Wait. You're telling me . . . Are those your *church* shoes?"

Cam shifted back and forth on the shoes in question. "I guess you could call them that."

Alex let out a hoot and shook his head. "Definitely something different."

Before Cam could think of a response, Alex was moving forward again, flipping a sultry look over his shoulder at Cam. "Come on, cowboy. Let's go exploring."

Cam wrung his hands and swallowed hard against the acidic, explosive feeling trying to race up out of his esophagus. The burning sensation had come back with a vengeance the second he'd stepped foot in Alex's apartment.

Alex had offered him a drink, but Cam had declined. Then Alex had excused himself to go to the bathroom, and Cam had been left alone in the living room, staring out at the skyline of Austin, with its myriad of twinkling lights. The place was decorated in sleek, modern lines—exactly the way Alex dressed. Cam wondered for a second whether Alex would wind up camouflaged if he sat down on the couch.

It was a nice place. Definitely one of the nicest apartments he'd ever seen. But it didn't feel particularly welcoming or relaxing, and that wasn't helping the twisting feeling in his gut.

He caught his reflection in the wall-to-wall windows, a blur of blue and shadow, and he moved closer to the shimmery image, pulled by some unknown motive.

That was when Alex came out of the bathroom, and Cam turned at the sound of the door clicking open to see him walk into the living room, holding something flat on his palm. Looked like a thin metal square with a funny pile of something on top.

"Great view, isn't it?" Alex jerked his chin toward the windows, but didn't bother waiting for an answer before setting the thing he was holding on the glass coffee table, looking up at Cam, and gesturing toward what Cam could now see was a small tray with a bunch of white powder on top. "Want some?"

Did he? Cam felt like the world's biggest idiot. He shoved his hands in his pockets to keep from scratching his head in confusion and looking like a complete yokel. "That depends. What is it?"

Alex laughed, and Cam tried not to cringe. It was a sweetly patronizing laugh, one that found innocence so novel as to be entertaining. Maybe, to some, the sentiment would be net positive, but the general indulgence with which Alex was treating him was starting to rankle.

None of which was helping the unsettled feeling in Cam's stomach.

"It's blow." Alex let out a truncated giggle before clarifying. "Cocaine, man."

"I don't under—" Cam's brain caught up. "It's drugs?"

His disapproval must have been more than clear in his tone, because Alex was now frowning.

"You gonna call the cops?" Alex sounded belligerent, and Cam's unease grew. A moment ago, the blond had been giggling. Now he seemed . . . tense. It felt alarmingly unnatural.

Cam shook his head. He felt sick. "No. But I have to go."

He started to walk toward the door, and Alex turned wheedling. "Hey, look, you don't have to do it. I can put it away. It was just to spice things up. Put a little extra edge in. You said you wanted something different."

Cam was already at the door, and half turned to answer. "It's—" he gestured toward the pile of white on the table "—more than that."

"What the fuck? You're leaving me like this?" Alex sneered. "I thought we were gonna fuck!"

Oh, sweet Jesus.

That definitely wasn't what he'd signed up for. "Thank you for having me over." Some stupid ingrained country-boy manners made him say it even as he flung the door open with so much force that it nearly hit the wall behind him, and stepped over the threshold.

"Fuck you, you cock-teasing hillbilly," Alex spat.

For a second, Cam hunched, thinking that everyone on the floor had just heard Cam McGhee being called out on his secret. But the periodically placed sconces provided enough light to prove that there was no one else out in the hallway at this time of night.

Who would know him here, anyway?

He didn't bother shutting the door behind him, but strode quickly toward the stairs next to the elevator, away from Alex, who was still standing in the doorway, backlit by that sleekly unwelcoming apartment. Cam pushed through the heavy fire door like a bulldozer and took the stairs two at a time. He burst out of the exit at the bottom, finding himself not in the lobby, but outside. A welcome relief. At least he wouldn't have to face the doorman in his jumbled-up state.

He kept walking swiftly for another block before it dawned on him that there was no reason to rush. Alex wasn't following him.

As he headed to the parking lot, his racing thoughts slowly calmed. By the time he reached his truck, his stomach felt back to normal too.

Well. Tonight certainly had been something different, though not in the way Cam had expected or hoped for. Alex had called him a *cock-tease*. Cam McGhee, the staid owner-operator of McGhee Feed & Grain, had been called something he never in his life expected to hear associated with his name.

He imagined the reaction from the guys at Rex's if word ever got out about what had happened tonight, and he couldn't help it. Shutting himself in the cab of his truck, he started to giggle, then realized he sounded exactly like Alex had. He was so keyed up that the thought made him explode into full-bodied laughter as he sat behind the wheel, until he'd laughed away the last of the nerves, started up the ignition, and drove away from this disaster of a night.

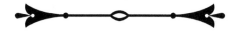

1979

Cam knew he had to stop watching Albert Clark, but he was having a hell of a time pulling his eyes away from the sweating, shirtless quarterback of their high school football team.

He had to stop taking risks, but it was as though his dick had a mind of its own.

It wasn't safe, though. He'd already been caught staring last week, when he'd been shoulder-punched by Trey Mooney and teasingly— *for now, so quit playing with fire*—called a homo. Cam had made his excuses, shaking his head and pretending he'd been spacing out, feigning that he'd registered nothing even though his eyes had been locked on the strong curve of Albert's back, skin so dark it shone purple under the hot Texas sun, thick thighs flexing, long calves straining—

"Hey, Cam."

Cam jerked his eyes away from where Albert was doing drills on the field. LaVerne Russo was standing next to the bench where Cam was sitting, her floral-patterned skirt billowing slightly in the breeze. *Uh-oh.* Had LaVerne noticed? She was a pleasant, pretty girl who tended to be a bit sickly, but had a generally sunny disposition despite her weak constitution and was friends with everyone.

He didn't think she'd try to get him in trouble, but what if she said something and it ended up all over the school?

Maybe no one would believe it.

But maybe they would.

"Hey, LaVerne." Cam stood up, remembering his manners somewhat belatedly, but LaVerne's smile was clearly forgiving. "Would you like to sit down?" He indicated the bench he'd just vacated and felt relieved when she nodded and smiled, sweeping a slender arm over her skirt before she settled onto the battered wooden seat.

Cam sat down at the other end, careful to leave some space between them. The town was too small to risk LaVerne's reputation by getting too close, but a part of him was overjoyed that others might see the two of them like this. That would be sure to put any potential rumors about his preferences at bay.

Unless LaVerne ended up starting those rumors.

You're being paranoid. Calm down and play it cool.

"How was your trip to Alamogordo?" he ventured. The Russos had driven out to New Mexico for spring break, and LaVerne had missed two days of school because of the vacation. It was all anyone could talk about, seeing as most folks around here didn't have enough money to get away that far for that long. But Mrs. Russo's sister lived in Alamogordo, and they'd stayed with her rather than spend too much on hotel lodging, which allowed everyone in town to continue being friendly—rather than soul-gnawing jealous—toward the Russos. As a result, everyone was asking for all the details about the trip. It was the safest topic Cam could think of.

"It was real nice. Thanks for asking." LaVerne was sitting slightly sideways, her gaze caught halfway between him and the field, and he could see her long brown fingers playing in the folds of her skirt. She was much lighter than her sister, but that might have been in part because LaVerne was often inside resting, rather than running around out of doors with the group of kids from their neighborhood.

"I'm glad to hear it."

What was she doing here? It wasn't out of the ordinary for her to talk to him—she lived three houses down, after all—but it was odd for her to approach him out of the blue like this, especially at football practice. Usually, he wouldn't even be available for her to chat with, since if he hadn't sprained his ankle last week, he'd be out on that field with the rest of them.

His throat felt dry as he waited, feeling the same way he did when Mama found out he'd done something wrong and he was waiting in his room for the punishment to be delivered.

"Cam?" She sounded nervous.

"Yup?" He *felt* nervous. Was she about to ask him why he'd been ogling Albert?

"Willyougotothedancewithme?"

Her words whooshed out on an exhale so fast that he had to take a few moments to process what she'd asked, but when realization finally dawned, he saw it for what it was.

A chance for safety.

"I'd love to," he told her with a smile. "How about I pick you up at six and we can walk over?"

Her inhale was loud—a long, nasal gasp—and she nodded her head with so much vigor that the thick plaits in her hair bounced up and down. "Sounds perfect."

And then she was rising, saying "Bye, Cam," and "See you Friday night." The guys on the field stopped what they were doing to watch her walk away, while Cam stared at Albert again and wondered if he'd just made the smartest decision or the biggest mistake of his young life.

Chapter Two

Cam stood on the balcony of his temporary apartment, sipping a cup of coffee and looking out over the parking lot of the complex.

This view was quite different from what he'd seen last night at Alex's.

Best be putting that out of your mind, now.

Through the glass sliding door, he heard the phone ring and he smiled. He enjoyed his early-morning peace, but as the only person who would be calling him at half past seven in the morning was Georgia, he gladly welcomed the interruption.

He stepped back inside, rolling the heavy door shut before grabbing up the phone from the wall just outside the kitchenette.

"This better be my daughter and not some telemarketer trying to sell me a timeshare," he laughed into the mouthpiece.

"How did you know it was me?" Georgia's voice was happy and soft, just like her mother's had been, and for a moment, Cam squeezed his eyes shut against a rush of pain and relief so intense that it nearly knocked the breath out of him.

Georgia isn't sick. She won't suffer like that.

Not like LaVerne had, especially in the last decade of her life.

When the diagnosis had first come back, Elijah was four years old and LaVerne was heavily pregnant with Georgia, experiencing trouble breathing, pain, and swelling beyond what seemed normal. When they'd gone in, Cam had been expecting advice like *eat better* or *make sure to rest more often*.

Instead, they'd found out that she had sickle cell anemia. The doctor had been shocked that LaVerne had managed to live as long as she had, and even more so that no one had diagnosed her before then. That kind of longevity wasn't completely unheard of, but back then most sufferers didn't live much past their teens, let alone up to their early thirties. That she managed to make it that long was a miracle in and of itself.

She'd gotten better care after that and finally passed last year of kidney failure at the age of fifty-four. The doctors had been astounded.

Everyone else had been devastated.

Both the kids had been tested at some point. Elijah hadn't inherited the gene, thank God, but Georgia was a carrier, and it scared the hell out of Cam.

"That's my secret," he answered, his grin falling fast and heavy into a serious straight line as soon as the word escape his mouth. Because of course that wasn't his *real* secret—the one that could ruin everything, from his entire business to these small, precious moments with his daughter.

He made himself smile again and asked, "What's up, honey? What do you need?"

There was a pause before she answered. "I don't need anything. I was just calling to say hi. See how you're doing."

He bit back a sigh. Ever since the funeral, the kids had been fussing over him, prodding him to talk about his feelings, to get away and take some time to think, even to go on dates.

With women.

They didn't realize. Not one danged thing.

"I'm doing all right." He lifted his free hand, only to realize he was still holding his mug of coffee. He took a sip.

"Cool."

Her tone belied her words, though. Cam could picture Georgia in her dorm room at SMU, where she was a senior—his little girl was graduating in a few months!—rolling her eyes at her dad's poor conversation skills.

Wouldn't be the first time.

"You still dating that good-for-nothing Evans boy?" He couldn't resist teasing her about her best friend every time they spoke on the phone. How many times had she insisted to Cam that she and Matt were "friends and nothing more"? And yet he'd seen the gleam in her eye when she talked about his accomplishments. How much she pined for him when she came home at Christmas break.

"Actually, there is something I was wondering," she told him.

He nearly laughed at her less-than-subtle change of topic. "What is it, honey?"

"Is it okay if I come visit you over spring break?"

His mouth twisted down for a second. Why would she want to come here? She and Elijah had finally gotten what they wanted—supposedly he was off doing whatever soul-searching they'd pushed him toward—and now she wanted to spend her time in a boring bachelor apartment?

But this was his daughter. It didn't matter why she wanted to come. It only mattered that he loved her and missed her and she would always be welcome in his home and heart. He liked to believe she felt the same about her old man.

It scared him to think that he might ever lose that love.

She could never know the truth.

He swallowed hard. "Sure, honey. You can come here. When is it?"

"Second week of March. You sure it's okay?"

Three weeks from now. Not that it mattered. He didn't have any plans, anyway. The next six months on his calendar were wide-open.

"It's fine. But why are you coming to visit your old man when you should be out having fun with your friends? I thought spring break was a time to party somewhere warm."

He hadn't been able to resist asking—just once.

"Maybe." She sounded tired. "It's my last year of school, and I probably should, but it feels kind of anticlimactic."

He took another sip of coffee. Somehow, it helped to focus him. "I understand. Well, come on down, then. I can't promise you anything too exciting, but I'll be glad to have you underfoot for a while."

She laughed. "Gee, thanks, Dad."

"I love you, honey."

"Love you too."

Cam hung up the phone and stood there for a long time before finally springing into action, heading to the shower and off to start his day in earnest.

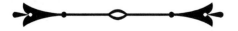

Cam stepped out of his apartment onto the landing. The place was a large, gated community of apartment blocks, twelve to each building, all stucco exterior and red-tile roofing. The front doors were placed off landings in open stairwells, making the entire thing look like an upscale roadside motel.

It wasn't his comfortable farmhouse back in Bitter, but it was nice enough.

He locked up and clomped down the stairs—he was wearing his yellow work boots today with jeans, which felt a hell of a lot more comfortable than the outfit he'd worn last night.

Church boots.

The whole getup, in fact, *was* what he usually wore to Sunday service. Alex had been dead on.

Cam reached his truck and shook his head in self-reproach as the night before replayed on fast-forward in his mind.

You're not supposed to be thinking about that.

But it had been too big a mistake to ignore completely.

Maybe this whole idea of "exploring" while he was in Austin wasn't such a good idea. He had a home, a business, two great kids. What more did he need? It wasn't as though a few months in the city were going to net him something life-changing.

Perhaps he simply wasn't meant to fill the last bit of empty space in his soul. He'd carried it with him his entire life, after all. It shouldn't make a difference for the next few decades.

Except . . . it was getting bigger, that emptiness. That was what had driven him to finally agree with his children to take a break—the growing *nothingness* inside of him that seemed to threaten to swallow him up soon if he didn't do something about it.

But how was he supposed to do this? He'd spent the past fifty years living a life he wasn't meant to have and now . . .

Well, now he had no idea who he was. Last night had been one big blunder. Proof enough that he wasn't sure which way was the right way.

Although, if there was one thing he *did* know for certain when he'd awoken this morning, it was that he'd made the right decision in the end. Of course, he couldn't go back to Ce-lo again—the bar he'd been in last night. He had a feeling it was a place Alex frequented with regularity, and Cam wasn't interested in repeating his mistakes.

He'd done that enough already for one lifetime.

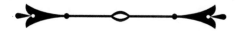

1980

His first time having sex with LaVerne, he'd closed his eyes and spent the entire time fantasizing about Albert Clark in order to get through it.

He'd known it was wrong. *So* wrong. He'd felt like a guilty, wretched mess afterward, as he'd lain next to LaVerne in the bed of his truck and held her close while she sighed and sniffled. He knew he'd hurt her physically, but she'd seemed overall pleased with the whole thing.

The sex itself had taken longer than it should have, and yet not long enough.

They'd been together over a year—since that Friday night dance she'd invited him to—and he'd been content to go along as they had been, with shared kisses and the occasional heavier sessions that always left him with an unpleasant feeling in his fingertips. But she'd surprised him last week, going on about how everyone was pairing up and "committing," which meant "having sex." Sex and commitment were the same thing in Bitter, anyway, unless you ran with the fast crowd.

LaVerne Russo was definitely not a member of the fast crowd.

Still, she'd been upset that they were the only ones who hadn't made the leap in their relationship. Hints had turned into a boldness with his body tonight that she hadn't shown before. Despite himself, he'd been aroused by her touch, and he'd closed his eyes to allow himself the small fantasy. Of *Albert* stroking down his chest. Albert rubbing him between his legs . . .

And then he'd let it go too far.

Oh, everyone else would be happy. Her parents were already overjoyed that she and Cam were together. His parents had practically sent out invitations to the wedding. He'd found himself having to remind them with increasing frequency that he and LaVerne had only started their senior year a couple of months ago. She'd just turned eighteen, for goodness' sake, and he wouldn't follow suit until April.

He should have realized sooner that none of that mattered. In the eyes of everyone in town, they were as good as hitched. If he walked out now . . .

Well, he wasn't that kind of guy.

No, you're the kind who uses a girl to hide behind.

Lying there, staring up at the starry sky, he felt the disgust roll through him at his own actions. He'd known all along that LaVerne was a safe bet. That going steady with her would keep the questions at bay. She talked just enough that people knew they were physically affectionate, but she didn't share all the details. People liked her. They trusted her, and by extension, they trusted him more too.

Now he'd hurt both of them.

But he'd had no choice. His mind whirred, trying to make sense of what he'd done.

You could have left town.

And gone where? How far would he have gotten without his family, too little education, no community to protect him?

No, he couldn't have left. And he didn't see himself living the rest of his life alone, like Mr. Armstrong. Cam wasn't sure whether the elderly man was gay or not, but he'd never married and there were no stories about him conducting any courtship. Cam didn't think it was a coincidence that Mr. Armstrong was a bitter, miserable man.

It made a guy wonder, anyway.

"Penny for your thoughts?" LaVerne's soft voice drifted over him in the darkness.

For a second, he stiffened, irrationally afraid she'd somehow heard what had been in his mind. Then he felt her hand gently rubbing his arm, and her lips dropped a kiss on his shoulder.

She's asking a simple question. Nothing more. She doesn't know your secret.

No one ever could. They'd run him out of town.

If they didn't kill him first.

He cleared his throat. "Just thinking about the future."

Her fingers skated down and laced in his. "Cam?"

"Yeah?"

"I love you," she whispered.

He closed his eyes. "I love you too."

That, at least, was true. He did love her, even if only as a friend. It wouldn't be so bad, would it? Spending forever with a friend.

She squeezed his hand, and he squeezed back, then once again lapsed into silence as he tried to get comfortable with his future.

Chapter Three

C am eased his truck into a parking space in front of the local coffee shop and cut the engine. He'd found this place the other day while exploring the neighborhood, and he'd taken a liking to the comfortable chairs, quiet hum of voices, and large windows with light-filtering shades. It was a welcoming place, like a man could come and stay awhile without bothering or being bothered.

He sauntered in and was paying for his coffee and a copy of the paper when a loud, masculine laugh caught his attention. Cam turned to see who had made such a bright sound . . .

White teeth against tanned skin . . .

The beat of his heart.

Short, dark-brown hair shot through with gray . . .

Time. Stopped.

It was every cliché—the laughing man pulling Cam's attention like a magnet—and yet it felt special, evoking memories of sitting shoulder to shoulder with Ray Nelson at an eighth-grade pep rally and the sheen of sunshine on Albert Clark's back. A sense of remembered anticipation filled Cam, accompanied by a very adult view of possibility. Tempered joy. Cautious hope.

"Sir?" A voice called him back to attention, and he jerked his head around to find the barista holding out his change. He pocketed the money sheepishly and scooped up the paper and his mug, intending to sit far away from that beautiful, joyous man, but for some fateful reason, the only available table was the one adjacent to the attractive stranger's.

Who, as Cam could see as he drew closer, was sitting with two other men who looked about the same age, all wearing bicycling gear.

Thin shirts. Tight shorts.

Cam's hand shook as he set his mug on the tabletop, the stoneware base clicking too hard against the wood. At the sound, the man's gaze flicked over to him for one overwhelming second. It was there and gone, barely even noticeable, but to Cam it felt like a tidal wave of stimulation.

His buckling knees had him practically dropping into the chair, and he immediately grabbed the front section of the paper he'd bought and opened it up wide. It was good to have a little cover while he surreptitiously checked out the man at the next table, whose black Spandex shorts showed off long, tanned legs, the lean muscles well-defined and complementary to the guy's wiry frame. A long-sleeved bike shirt—white with a simple red logo on the front—completed the outfit, and a pair of fingerless gloves sat discarded atop a phone on the table's polished wood surface.

Studying him up close, Cam could see that the other man wasn't actually beautiful. Probably no one would ever suggest he could be a magazine model or a leading actor. But there was something about him that Cam couldn't get enough of. The small lines around his eyes, his slender build and welcoming face that added a youthful vibe Cam wanted for himself, through this man. *In* this man.

This is what it's supposed to feel like. This is what you've wanted your entire life.

The revelation smacked him in the frontal cortex just as the stranger turned his head again, as if sensing someone watching him, and Cam started, whipping his gaze back down to the newspaper, unable to process that last thought past the burning in his cheeks.

Dang, he'd got caught. He shifted uncomfortably, hoping the stranger would ignore the weird moment and give Cam time to leave without it being too obvious that he was actually fleeing out of embarrassment.

Slowly, he began to fold up the paper, his movements purposely deliberate, when the stranger spoke.

"Excuse me."

Sweet Jesus, he's talking to you.

So much for making a quiet exit.

The man he'd just been ogling leaned over and braced one long-fingered, sinewy hand on Cam's table for balance. *Wow*, that was a beautiful hand. Images swam in his mind of possible actions that hand could take—things he'd seen right after LaVerne died, when he'd been weak and vulnerable enough to go hunting around on the internet for stimulation. He'd kept himself from doing it for all the years of his marriage, knowing it would be a way of cheating on a woman he was already hurting so much with his lack of attraction.

But now those images he'd stared at months ago were pouring back into his waking mind, and as a result, blood was congregating in Cam's nether regions, giving him the start of a rather unprecedented public erection.

Aw, man. Where were the signs of aging when he needed them? This kind of thing hadn't happened since high school.

Cam folded the front section completely, exposing his nerves directly to the power of the stranger's handsome face, and gave what he hoped was a politely inquiring look. He didn't trust himself to speak for fear his voice would crack on top of everything else, while beneath the cover of the table, he slowly crossed his legs, hiding his increasingly prominent bulge.

The man flashed him a brilliant smile. "Do you mind if I borrow this section for a bit?" His beautiful fingers were now resting atop the Business pages.

Cam shook his head. "Don't mind." He managed something between a whisper and a normal speaking voice, making the words come out at a raspy, unnatural volume.

You sound like a B-movie bad guy.

"Thanks." The Business section started to slide away from Cam, but then stopped. "I'm Dave, by the way. Dave Montoya."

The hand was lifting, being offered up for a shake. To Cam's mind, it was infinitely more pornographic than any of the photos and videos he'd viewed months ago.

He cleared his throat and reached out to grip Dave's hand in his.

Warm palms touching.

Strong fingers wrapping.

Even the *size* of Dave's hand felt good.

"Cam McGhee," he managed to reply.

"Nice to meet you." And then Dave was pulling away, scooping up the paper with another "Thanks," and turning back to his companions, who were finishing up their coffees and making desultory conversation. They appeared to be winding down.

Cam went back to pretending to read the paper, needing to wait until his arousal abated before he risked standing up and leaving. Not two minutes later, Dave's two companions stood and pulled on their biking gloves, shook hands with Dave, and clopped out of the café on their bike shoes.

Over the top of his paper, Cam watched them walk out the door, and when he brought his eyes back to the table where they'd been sitting, he found Dave watching *him*, the borrowed Business section draped over his lap.

"I think our generation is the last one that doesn't read the paper online," he remarked.

For a second, Cam merely stared dumbly, but fortunately some latent recognition that someone was speaking to him and it was impolite not to respond kicked him into action.

"Maybe." He focused on the fact that he talked to other men all the time—men back in Bitter that he'd found sort of appealing, even—and never had a problem acting normal.

You knew those men were off limits, though. You were off limits.

Who said Dave wasn't off limits too, though? For all Cam knew, Dave could be completely straight. Married. A priest. And still Cam found his tongue getting trapped in his mouth.

You are fifty-four years old. You've run a good business for over three decades. Talk, for God's sake.

"I think . . ." he noticed that Dave had light-brown eyes the color of honey wine ". . . it has more to do with disposable income than age when it comes to the younger generations," he finished.

Dave nodded. "Good point." He casually tossed the paper onto the table in front of him, turning completely toward Cam. Giving Cam his full attention.

Oh, Lord, what have I done?

Cam's heartrate sped up so much that he noticed it through a near-painful throbbing in the veins on the back of his hand.

"Out where I'm from, internet at home still isn't all too common. Most folks, old and young, get their news from the paper. Or the TV. Everything is spread out and the infrastructure to get connected is expensive. You can't develop a habit when the bits and bobs you need to support it don't exist."

How embarrassing. He'd gone from tongue-tied to babbling, and Dave had done nothing more than strike up a casual conversation in a coffee shop. Something strangers did all the time, every day, all over the country.

"Where are you from?" Dave asked.

And now he'd set himself up to have to share more information than he wanted to. Alex had asked the same thing last night, and Cam had managed to avoid answering, but somehow he didn't think it would work as well on Dave.

Well, no . . . it *would* work. Dave would certainly get the hint and withdraw.

But Cam didn't want him to.

"Bitter." Saying it made him feel exposed and relieved at the same time. "West of San Angelo."

"I don't know it." Dave shrugged almost apologetically. "Are you just visiting Austin, then?"

Was it Cam's over-hopeful imagination, or did Dave seem disappointed at the possibility that Cam was just passing through?

"I'm here for six months. A long visit, I suppose you could say."

No. It wasn't his imagination. Dave visibly brightened, flashing one of those lovely white grins his way.

It was a heady rush.

"Well, how about that." Dave reached back, picked up the Business section, and returned it to the table in front of Cam. "Didn't realize how late it was already. I have to head off, but thanks for the loan."

Dave rose while Cam's shoulders dropped in disappointment. He forced a smile and looked up, shutting his senses against how tall Dave was. Masculine. Imposing.

Off limits.

At least, it wasn't gonna happen, which amounted to the same thing.

"No problem," Cam croaked out. "You have a good one."

Dave scooped up his gloves and phone, then nodded down at Cam. "You too. Maybe I'll see you around. I ride with those guys every Saturday morning, and we usually end up here when we finish."

That sounded like an invitation.

Cam smiled. "I guess I'll see you around, then."

Dave gave him a funny little salute, then turned and headed toward the door while Cam once again opened his newspaper. He still hadn't read a word.

But he enjoyed the view he got around the edges of the newsprint as he watched Dave walk away.

Two days later, Cam had just finished lunch and was sitting at his small dinette table, thumbing through a catalog for the local adult education center, when the phone rang. He twisted in his seat and grabbed it from the hook, fighting the bizarre hope that Dave had somehow waited outside the coffee shop until Cam left, followed him to the supermarket and for a walk around the park, then back to his apartment, then somehow managed to figure out his phone number based on his address.

Except that whole scenario would be . . . not a point in Dave's favor.

He pressed the phone to his ear. "Hello?"

"Hey, Dad."

"Elijah. Hey, son. I haven't heard from you in the last twenty-four hours. I was starting to worry," he teased. With Elijah covering for him back at the feed store, they talked almost daily about various aspects of the business.

Elijah gave a laughing groan. "Funny, Dad. As usual. Listen, I was talking to Aunt Patrice today, and she said something I thought you might want to hear."

Cam allowed himself a small eye roll. He loved LaVerne's older sister—they'd grown up together too—but sometimes she didn't know when to keep her mouth shut. There was always something Cam "might want to hear" whenever Patrice was involved.

"Is it about Reverend Smith again?" Patrice loved to criticize the new preacher at their church over every little thing. Poor man had the patience of a saint.

A crackle came through the phone that sounded like a hard puff of air, then Elijah's amused voice followed. "No. This time she was going on about how much she misses you, and how she can't wait for the six months to be over. How the town isn't the same without you, and so you never should have been damn fool enough to have left here in the first place."

Cam sighed. That woman was an expert in backhanded compliments.

"I'm sorry you had to deal with that because of me," he said, but Elijah stopped him.

"I don't mind. But that's not the whole thing. After she said that, she started saying she thinks you might be dating someone in Austin and was asking me if I knew anything about it."

Cam froze, panicking despite himself. There was no way Patrice could know that he'd been in a gay bar last Friday night—had gone home with a man, even if nothing had really happened. There was no way she could know that he had also been flirting with a different man two mornings ago.

But it didn't stop the familiar fear flooding through him that someone might find him out at any moment. He'd told Dave he was from Bitter, for goodness' sake. It was possible. And if anyone back home found out, that'd be it. He wouldn't be able to go back. Elijah would be snubbed by too many closed-minded folks. The business would suffer, maybe even fold.

He gripped the phone with both hands. "I'm not dating anyone." That was true, at least.

"I know. I mean, Lord knows how many times I've tried to get you to meet new people, and all you do is refuse. But she went by the house yesterday afternoon to dust the place and said she found your wedding ring in a drawer."

Cam should have been relieved that an unworn ring was the only thing fueling Patrice's curiosity about his love life. But even if it hadn't been, the disappointment in Elijah's voice would have trumped every other worry.

"Elijah . . ."

"It's okay, Dad. It's your business. Caught me by surprise, is all. I assumed you were still wearing it in Austin."

He should have brought it here, at least. Not left it lying around for Patrice to find.

Who dusts inside a drawer, anyway?

However, the idea that he should have brought it here, only to leave it in the cheap MDF dresser in the bedroom, felt worse somehow. He thought about what that ring meant and knew it had been right to leave it back in Bitter, but he wished he could have spared Elijah the hurt.

"I'm sorry, son. I didn't mean to upset you. I hadn't intended to wear it the rest of my life, but I had meant to set down and talk to you about it too. Face-to-face. You shouldn't have found out that way."

"Dad," Elijah started but then stopped for a moment. Cam imagined his son looking up at the sky and just *breathing*, like he tended to do when he was feeling overwhelmed. A second later, Elijah continued, "It really is okay. It's been almost a year, and Mom was in bad shape for a long time before then. It's just . . . well, it will be nice to have you back come July. I'll try not to drive the shop into the ground before then."

Cam could sense Elijah didn't want to discuss it anymore. Just like his old man in that respect. He'd said his piece and it was time to move on.

"I'm sure you won't. You've been doing such a good job already that it seems to me like I won't have anything left to do when I come back."

"Maybe you should take up a hobby so you have something to occupy your time when you get back home," Elijah teased.

Cam's gaze fell on the open catalog he'd been looking through when Elijah had called.

Telling Your Story: Putting your own hopes, dreams, and experiences in writing.

Maybe . . . next session.

"There's an embroidery class at the adult education center," he told Elijah, who laughed.

"Make me something pretty." Elijah's happiness eased the ache in Cam's chest. "I gotta run, Dad. I'll talk to you soon."

They said their good-byes, and Cam hung up the phone, then sat back down at the table, thinking over the short conversation. Elijah was right: LaVerne had been sick for a long time before she died. They'd all started hinting months ago that they'd understand if he needed a little female company. No one suspected that the company he really wanted was the kind he'd been denying himself his entire life.

He didn't think Elijah would react in the same accepting way if Cam dropped that bomb on him anytime soon.

Maybe next session.

Maybe never.

Cam sighed and went back to browsing through the catalog.

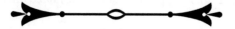

1981

LaVerne had been tired lately. Not surprising, with final exams and all the wedding preparations she'd been dealing with. Cam had tried to help wherever he could, but it hadn't made much of a difference. She'd been too worn out to spend much time with him in the past month. Still, he dropped by her house every day and sat with her in the den or outside in the garden if the weather was fine. They would graduate in another week and be married less than two weeks after that.

A small, horrible part of him was relieved, though, that LaVerne was too exhausted to see him at night, when he might have felt pressured to have sex with her. Since their first time, it had been infrequent, and she'd seemed content with that, but now it was nonexistent.

A reprieve.

He was walking home on a Thursday afternoon, trudging down the sun-baked dirt road leading out of the high school, when the reality hit him.

This was the rest of his life.

Despite the Stetson perched atop his shorn head, the sweat rolling down his neck and into the collar of his worn Western button-down, a chill gripped him, and he stumbled, scuffing the toe of his left boot before managing to right himself.

The sound of an engine slowing behind him caught his attention, and he turned in time to see Albert Clark leaning one arm on the sill of the rolled-down window of his beat-up old Ford, the other hand barely keeping the truck on course.

"I saw you're having some trouble walking," Albert teased. "Need a ride?"

And then . . . he *winked* at Cam.

Cam's heart flipped over at the flirty gesture.

No. Not flirty. He's not flirting. He's being friendly because he's a guy and you're a guy and he thinks you're not *interested in kissing him.*

Cam made himself dial back his urge to smile like a besotted fool. "Hey, Albert. Yeah, I'd appreciate a ride." He huffed out a laugh. "Sure is hot out today."

"It's May. What'd you expect?" Albert snorted, came to a complete stop, and jerked his thumb toward the passenger's side. "Hop on in."

Cam practically sprinted around the front of the truck to launch himself in the cab alongside Albert, shutting the door behind him and trying not to swoon at the smell of the other young man, a mix of soap, sweat, and sun-soaked outdoors.

Albert gunned the engine, and they took off, careening down the road, wind whipping through the open windows. Cam found himself laughing at Albert's wild streak.

"You got time to go mudding? The old quarry is still good for a few more weeks."

Racing through a muddy track, watching the splotches of wet earth fly, the speed and the dirt and Albert . . .

Cam reluctantly shook his head. "I've got to stop in and see LaVerne."

"How's she doing? Feeling better?" Albert slowed the truck when he asked it, as though exhibiting some sort of funny vehicular respect.

Cam nodded. "Improving every day. Since her mom and my mom started picking up the wedding stuff, she's got a lot more energy. She'll probably be completely back to her usual self after the weekend."

"Good to hear it. Y'all's wedding is all the girls can talk about these days. Hannah won't let up on me about when we're gonna have a turn."

Cam didn't miss how Albert's hand tightened on the steering wheel.

"So *is* it gonna happen anytime soon?" he asked. Better to be straightforward than try to tiptoe around things when it came to Albert.

Albert sighed. "Probably. I mean, yeah, it will. I can't hold off much longer than a year, anyway, without causing a fuss. But sometimes . . ."

Cam wasn't sure whether Albert was lost in thought or simply didn't want to share the rest of that sentence, so he stayed silent. Waiting, even though he wanted to poke and prod and find out what Albert had been about to say.

Thankfully, he didn't have to wait long. After a few seconds of distracted driving, Albert picked up where he'd left off. "I think about taking off and going up to Dallas for a little bit. Just to see what it's like before I settle down and turn into one of the old men who sit around Rex's joint all day. Not run away, but just . . . get away. You know?"

I do know.

Albert sighed. "I want to do it. But I'm waiting for a good time to spring it on Hannah. Maybe right after your wedding I can tell her that I want to go for a month or two and then when I'm back, we can get married."

Take me with you.

Cam's reasons were different from Albert's, though. Cam wanted to go with *Albert* as much as he wanted to get away from this town in general. But even then, he had a sneaking suspicion that if he ever left, he'd never be able to come back. What would become of him then?

He needed this town and the people in it. His future depended on him being able to fit in. Not only his future—LaVerne's, too. He was responsible for someone else now.

It felt unbearably heavy, that responsibility.

The talk turned to football, and before Cam knew it, Albert was pulling up in front of LaVerne's place.

"This is your stop." Albert threw the truck into Park and turned to give Cam a friendly shoulder punch, accompanied by a wide smile. "Not even married and you're already letting her lead you around by the nose."

Cam had been so relaxed, talking about everyday things and letting the hot wind rush over his body, soothing him into a state of ease, he wasn't prepared for the onslaught of sensation that Albert's smile spurred back to the surface.

He had to get out of here before he did something stupid, like lean over and kiss his friend.

Well, make an attempt to kiss him, anyway.

Because Albert would never let you actually put your lips on his. You'd get beat down so fast, you wouldn't even see it coming.

Cam let out a nervous chuckle. "Thanks for the ride." He was grateful for the excuse to turn away and grabbed the door handle, pushed the door open, and swung his whole body out of the truck.

He slammed the door behind him, and Albert threw out a, "See you 'round!" before speeding off.

Cam was walking up the front path when the door opened and Mrs. Russo appeared on the doorstep.

"Was that the youngest Clark boy?" She peered up the road, but the truck was already out of sight.

"Yes, ma'am. Albert," Cam answered, coming to a stop before the Russo matriarch.

"Takes after his father," she commented, her mouth drawing tight as she continued looking at the empty intersection at the top of their street.

Cam wasn't sure what to say to that—he didn't know in what way Albert resembled Mr. Clark other than sharing the same square jawline—so he kept silent, and after a second Mrs. Russo turned back to him and smiled warmly.

"Well. Enough of that. Come on in, Cam. LaVerne's feeling back to normal today and is looking forward to sitting outside with you."

Cam followed Mrs. Russo, but just before he stepped over the threshold of his fiancée's home, he turned and looked up the street too.

Empty.

Opportunity gone.

He shook his head at himself and went inside, shutting the door behind him.

Chapter Four

That Saturday morning, Cam was already sitting at the coffee shop, newspaper spread over his table, when Dave and his two friends walked in.

Cam had looked up at the sound of male voices, and his eyes had locked on Dave's immediately. Dave smiled and gave a nod of greeting before turning his attention back to his friends.

Cam went back to his paper, but his heart was racing.

Dave had been *looking* for him. Seeking him out. And he'd seemed happy to see that Cam was here.

Did that mean he was attracted to Cam, though? Or just being friendly?

Lord save me. I have no idea how to do this.

He read the paper and sipped his coffee while the cyclists got their drinks, and by the time the three other men arrived at the table next to him—he did notice that Dave had walked slightly ahead of the others and seemed to be the one to choose the table right by Cam, though that could be because it was the same place they'd sat last week—Cam was feeling jumpy.

This is not a big deal. Just two men getting friendly.

He barely suppressed a groan at the thought, which sounded overtly sexual to his excited mind.

"Morning, Cam. Good to see you here again." Dave bent to set his drink and phone down. It was unseasonably warm today, and this time Dave was in short sleeves. His forearms flexed and rippled as he began to pull off his gloves.

Cam managed to utter a return greeting, but his throat was feeling awfully dry from watching such a sexy man strip those stretchy things off his hands and fingers. All while standing so close that Cam could smell the soap-and-sweat scent of him.

Cam couldn't stop his eyes from skimming down Dave's body, taking in the wiry arms, taut chest, flat stomach, lean hips, tight shorts that revealed—

Oh my goodness.

Cam felt his cheeks heat and jerked his eyes back to Dave's face.

Dave was *smirking.*

For a second, all Cam could do was blink and frown. It was almost as though Dave had been doing all that *posturing* on purpose, to get Cam to—

Oh.

Oh.

Dave was interested.

Or if not really *interested*, he was at least flirting.

With Cam.

Cam could feel his eyes widening and his mouth opening slightly. He must look like such a green boy, but Dave didn't seem to mind. In fact, he held Cam's gaze as he dropped his gloves atop his phone and slid into his seat.

"How was your week?" Dave's voice sounded a bit lower than usual, the sound pinning Cam under the weight of his own arousal.

"Yep. Good." Cam could barely grunt out a response. "Yours?"

Dave smiled, but it wasn't what Cam would call *friendly*. It was a smile of satisfaction—the kind a man wore when he was getting what he wanted.

Which meant—well, it seemed to mean, anyway—that Dave wanted *Cam*.

Cam felt suddenly lightheaded. Little yellow spots were dancing in his field of vision and he feared he might actually pass out from euphoria.

"It was a busy one." Dave's friends also dropped their phones and gloves on the table, smoothing bare fingers through sweat-spiked hair before sitting down as well, and Cam took the opportunity to turn away, making a show of picking up his spoon and stirring his coffee, though the milk hadn't separated one bit in the past two minutes.

He shook the spoon twice, set it back on the napkin where he'd left it originally, and took a calming sip.

By the time the bustle had settled, so had Cam's nerves.

"I technically retired two years ago," Dave explained, "but I still do consulting work and recently took on a new project, so the hours have been longer than I'm used to."

Cam set the mug back down, feeling notably more in control of himself. At least enough to look at Dave again.

Thank God the man was wearing a fairly neutral expression. Maybe he'd realized he was unnerving Cam.

"What kind of consulting?"

"Software development. Well, more on the management side, but in the industry, anyway."

Cam searched for something to say. He didn't know much about software. He knew what it was, but it wasn't his area of expertise by a long shot. Luckily, he was saved by one of Dave's friends.

"I still can't believe companies pay you that much money to give lessons in common sense." The man snorted, pulling Dave's attention away from Cam for a moment.

"You're one to talk," Dave shot back, but he was laughing as he said it.

Dave looked over at Cam. "This is Pedro Tijeras, my biggest critic," he said, pointing to the man who'd just spoken. Pedro had a broad face, high cheekbones, and a wide, flat nose. His face matched the rest of his build—a square build on a medium-height frame. "And this is Richard Rhys." The third man looked mixed, tall and muscular with light-brown skin and light eyes. He seemed slightly younger than the other two, but his face tended toward a more solemn expression. "This is Cam McGhee," Dave finished, gesturing toward Cam, who inclined his head in recognition.

"Good to meet y'all both." He reached out a hand and leaned forward, Pedro and Richard each giving him a solid shake in turn.

"Cam's new in town," Dave told them. "He's visiting for a while from Bitter."

Cam flinched slightly at the public announcement.

"I've heard of Bitter," Richard commented. "It's a black farm town, right?"

Cam nodded slowly, feeling reluctant to confirm more details but recognizing how strange it would look if he avoided the question. "It's not a well-known place."

Richard shook his head. "I'd imagine not. But there was an article a few months back in *Texas Today*, talking about the disappearance of all-African-American towns in recent years, and they mentioned Bitter as one of the remaining ones."

Please talk about something else.

Dave laughed. "Richard never forgets anything he sees. Photographic memory, that one."

"I wish I had that talent," Cam remarked, and Pedro nodded in agreement.

Richard shook his head. "You wouldn't be saying that if you couldn't get some of the images I've seen out of your mind."

The three cyclists grew quiet for a moment, until Pedro spoke up, explaining, "Richard was an Associated Press correspondent for decades, through a couple of the Middle East wars."

Ah. That explained the gravity of his expression and the moment of seriousness.

Cam slowly nodded his head, acknowledging without words the struggles Richard undoubtedly must have witnessed. "Are you still a journalist?"

Richard shrugged. "Not the same, but yes. I do mostly long-form stuff now. Essays, stories around sociological research, that kind of thing."

They'd probably all gone to college, these men. But they spoke to him like they didn't care about his relative lack of education, and after another half hour of conversation, Cam found himself believing that they didn't care that he was attracted to men, either.

Pedro was the first to take off, telling them he had a surgery scheduled for later that afternoon—he was a cardiothoracic surgeon who was apparently so sought-after that he could make his own schedule—and shook Cam's hand good-bye with what sounded like a genuine wish to see him again.

Richard left shortly after that. He didn't give a reason, but judging from the looks he was giving Cam and Dave, Cam had a sneaking suspicion that Richard wanted to give them some time alone, as though he *wanted* Cam and Dave to get together.

It was such a foreign feeling—the support of others for who he was—that Cam hadn't expected to experience. He'd come to Austin thinking he'd kiss a man or two, maybe go a little further. But this . . .

This felt a lot like building the start of a *life*. A whole self.

It scared the hell out of him.

But before he could process any more thoughts around that fear, Dave leaned forward, resting his elbows on his knees, and leveled Cam with a look of such intensity that fear simply wasn't an option at that moment.

"Cam." Dave's voice matched his look. Intense. Serious. "I think it's probably obvious that I find you attractive. And if I'm reading things right, you think the same thing about me."

Well, that was direct.

Not like how Alex was direct, though. It wasn't a proposition. It wasn't even very sexual.

Cam liked it.

He nodded. "You're right. I do think the same thing."

Dave smiled, his face relaxing significantly, as though he'd been tense before Cam had admitted his own feelings.

Had Dave been nervous?

Cam nearly laughed at the idea. Dave came across as so confident in his own desires.

"I'm glad to hear it," Dave said. "Because I was wondering if you'd like to go out with me. Maybe tomorrow evening?"

Jesus help me.

He'd just been asked out on a date by a man he found attractive. A date. Not hooking up or sex or anything similarly casual and meaningless. He wasn't sure whether to be thrilled or wary. This was getting into a much more serious realm than he'd planned to explore while in the city, but at the same time, he didn't think he was any good at the kind of exploring Alex had proposed last week.

Well, whatever you do, do not start hyperventilating.

Dave was looking at him expectantly.

Dave was a nice man with kind, educated, open-minded friends. And . . .

Do you need any more reasons?

"Yes," he told Dave. "I'd love to."

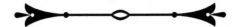

Cam thumbed through a rack of shirts in the men's section of one of the big department stores at the mall. He'd driven there right after he and Dave had parted ways at the coffee shop, which had been after they'd made arrangements for when (seven o'clock) and where (Cam's apartment) to meet the following evening. Dave had been bewildered that Cam had neither cell phone nor internet, but at least he didn't make Cam feel like an adorably naïve poster child for the Middle Ages.

Still, Cam was determined not to go to his grave angry over being too quaint to kiss. His time in Austin was his only chance to have this experience, and he didn't want to blow it.

"Is there anything I can help you with, sir?"

A saleswoman had approached him from the side, and Cam turned to look at her, barely containing a grimace when he realized that she looked eerily similar to LaVerne's sister Patrice.

"No, I—" he started to decline, feeling awkward about asking a Patrice lookalike to help him dress for a first date with another man, but the urge to impress Dave won out. He shook himself and nodded, instead. "Yes, actually. I need some clothes for a . . . um . . . an event. I'm not sure what to wear. I haven't been shopping in years."

"I see." She nodded politely. "What kind of event is it? Formal, semiformal?"

He coughed once, shifting on his feet. Maybe this wasn't such a good idea.

"Do you need to wear a suit?" she followed up, probably sensing his discomfort. She seemed kind. Subtle. Not like Patrice.

He started to shake his head, then shrugged. "I don't know." *May as well admit you're out of your element.* "It's actually a date."

"Oh!" The saleswoman's eyes lit up. "How lovely. Well, where are you taking her?"

Actually, he's *taking* me *somewhere.*

But he couldn't say that. He didn't feel bold enough. And— Oh, sweet Jesus, did that mean he was the girl in this scenario? He'd never thought about that.

He fumbled past the sudden wrench in his brain, searching for the name of the place Dave had mentioned earlier when they'd been making plans.

"The Cotton Lounge?" He wasn't completely sure he'd gotten the name right.

But the Patrice doppelgänger seemed to take his uncertainty for a need for validation. She nodded. "Great choice. Upscale but casual and comfortable. I'd say slacks and a button-down, or maybe a light sweater over an undershirt. The nights are still cool enough that you could do a blazer if you wanted, but it's not necessary."

Uh . . . okay.

He understood about half the words that had just come out of her mouth, but she seemed confident. Cam figured he'd let her take charge on this one.

"Sounds good. Do you mind making a few choices? It would be real nice if things were on sale too," he added. No use wasting her time chasing down things that were too expensive.

Not that he didn't have the money.

Decades without a cell phone or internet can add up to a lot of savings.

He smiled at his own thoughts, but she must have thought he was smiling at her, because she returned the expression and winked. "No problem." She held out her hand. "I'm Darlene, by the way."

He shook her hand. "Cam."

"Well, Cam, nice to meet you. Why don't you come along with me and we'll choose a few things you can start with?" Darlene gestured for him to follow her and started walking away without bothering to wait for an answer.

An hour later he left the shop, bag in hand. He was going to look good tomorrow. He hoped Dave would think so too. It was the first time Cam had new clothes this nice since his wedding.

With a little luck, though, tomorrow night would be nothing like the day he'd gotten married.

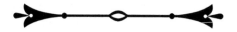

1981

LaVerne walked down the aisle of First Presbyterian, wearing a dress that had taken her mother two months to make and all the women had been talking about as "breathtakingly gorgeous," and the only thing Cam could think was, *This isn't right*.

If he left the church now, jumped into the truck Dad and Mom had given him as a wedding present, and didn't bother to stop for clothes or cash or any of that at home, he could be out of here and in Dallas or Austin by early evening.

Dallas or Austin? Dallas was much more metropolitan, but Austin had more hippies. Dallas? Getting lost in the anonymity of the city? Or Austin and free love and acceptance in a smaller community?

"Who gives this woman's hand in marriage?"

Reverend Mooney—the father of Cam's friend Trey—boomed out the question so close to Cam's ear that he jumped in surprise, making the congregation laugh.

Cam cast a sheepish look at LaVerne, but fortunately she was giggling along with everyone else.

"I do," Mr. Russo said around a grin, and in the next moment, he was handing LaVerne over to Cam, shaking with one hand while patting Cam on the back with the other.

"No need to be nervous, son," he whispered to Cam. "We're all on your side."

And then Mr. Russo was walking away, Reverend Mooney was starting the ceremony, and Cam was cringing under the feeling of being watched by hundreds of good citizens of Bitter, turned out in their Sunday finery for the most romantic wedding they'd seen in years.

He didn't pretend not to know what they'd been saying: that it was so sweet and fitting that kind, earnest Cam McGhee had fallen in love with a weak little thing like LaVerne. Cam could be trusted to care for her because Cam was honest and forthright and sensitive enough to understand LaVerne's needs.

But they had it all wrong. He wasn't doing anything special for LaVerne—well, okay, maybe he was. But that was incidental. Mostly, he was giving her his problems and she would be his sanctuary.

It wasn't right. But he had to make it so. He would. Even if it meant denying the one thing he wanted more than all others.

Up there in front of God and the gossips, Cam had never felt more alone.

Chapter Five

On Sunday evening, Cam was standing in his small living room, unable to sit from nerves, when the bell rang. He looked through the window cut in the wall adjoining the kitchen to check the clock on the stove back.

Exactly seven o'clock.

It made Cam smile. He appreciated when people were on time.

Cam smoothed his hands down his sweater—Darlene had picked out a light-brown Merino wool one with lavender accents, though for the life of him he couldn't see any lavender anything—and strode to the door.

He opened it and nearly stopped breathing.

Dave was standing on the other side wearing a boyish grin, charcoal-gray slacks, and a black button-down. Cam had never seen him in anything other than bicycling clothes, and the outfit he wore now enhanced his lean figure and made the chiseled features of his face stand out.

"Dave. Hi." The words came out on a *whoosh*, feeling jittery and delighted and uncertain.

Dave gave him one of those beautiful big grins in return. "Hey, Cam. You look great."

"Thanks." Cam felt himself blushing. "So do you."

Dave held out his arms to his sides, showing off his clothes. "Believe it or not, it's more comfortable than bike shorts." He laughed, clearly oblivious to the fact that all the blood in Cam's body was rushing toward his groin. "Ready to go?"

Cam gritted his teeth, trying to focus on mundane things. It wasn't easy to walk with half an erection. "Yep." He stepped outside, closer to Dave, who moved back only slightly, which left them standing within inches of one another as Cam turned back to lock the door behind him.

Dave smelled different today. Still amazing, but the scent of sweat and outdoors was gone. Now it was soap and aftershave and freshly pressed fabric.

They walked side by side, Dave subtly guiding them toward a sleek black BMW parked in the visitor's space in front of Cam's building. Cam went around to the passenger's-side door, relieved that Dave wasn't insisting on opening the door for him. For some reason, it was too big a leap for Cam to take on top of everything else.

Dave pulled out of the complex and turned toward the highway, the car easing on with a barely noticeable surge of power. Quite a difference from Cam's old truck.

But he loved his old truck.

"Have you been to the Cotton Lounge yet?" Dave asked, glancing over at Cam for a second.

Cam shook his head even though Dave's attention had already turned back to the road. "I've only been in Austin for two weeks, actually. I've been walking a lot, getting to know the lay of the land, but the only places I've gone to so far are the grocery store, the coffee shop, and a place called Ce-lo."

Dave made a slight choking sound. "You went to Ce-lo?"

Cam didn't miss the surprise in his tone. "Yeah. But it wasn't really my scene, turns out." He conveniently pushed thoughts of Alex to the back of his mind. No use sharing that particular humiliating debacle.

Dave flipped on his signal to exit. "I can't say I'm shocked to hear that, though I admit I'm curious why you went to the city's most infamous gay bar. You don't seem the type."

Cam laughed. There was no real judgment in Dave's words, but it was clear that Dave wasn't the type to frequent Ce-lo, either. "I figured that out, in the end. Not as quickly as I should have, which makes me feel sort of stupid, but I don't see myself returning there, ever."

Dave frowned as he approached the stoplight at the end of the access road, taking the opportunity while they were stopped to turn and look at Cam. "You're not stupid."

It was said with so much conviction, so much *faith*, that Cam had to look away.

The light changed, and the car went forward again but slowed as they came up on an entrance to a shopping center. "Who told you to go there, anyway?"

Cam gave a small cough. "I, uh, I looked it up online."

"Did it have any reviews? Tips from locals?"

"It might have. But . . ." *Oh, Lord.* "My son came in the room while I was looking it up, and I had to close the browser real quick. I thought I had everything I needed."

The answering silence as Dave pulled the car into an empty space in the lot outside the restaurant was pensive. Cam tensed.

Dave put the car in Park and cut the engine, then twisted toward Cam, sliding one arm behind the passenger's seat and leaning in a little. "You have a kid."

Cam nodded. "Two kids. Elijah is twenty-six and Georgia is twenty-two."

Dave's eyebrows went up. "Are they adopted?" He gave a half shrug and added, "That is, if I may ask."

Cam felt like he was about to confess a dark, terrible secret. "I was married." He watched Dave's face carefully, but the other man didn't so much as blink. "For thirty-five years."

Cam started counting the seconds of silence. One, two, three, four, five, six, seven . . .

Dave *finally* blinked. "You were married. To a woman, I suppose. I don't think anything but heterosexual marriage was legal thirty-five years ago."

Cam nodded and swallowed, his throat feeling unpleasantly tight. "Yes. To a woman. My wife, uh, she died of kidney failure. Sickle cell anemia. It eventually destroyed her organs. She was bedridden for months toward the end."

His voice broke a little, and he immediately stopped, feeling even more wrong-footed. He hadn't meant to say anything about Elijah and Georgia just yet, and certainly he hadn't even considered mentioning LaVerne in the first twenty minutes of the date. Yet somehow he'd found himself not only spilling everything, but now he was sharing too much.

Too much, too depressing, too—

Dave sat back, blowing out a long breath. "Hey. Wow. Cam, I'm sorry. I didn't mean to grill you, there. The having-kids thing took me by surprise because I didn't realize you're bi, but I shouldn't have let it blow up like that and stir up sad memories. Not a great way to start an evening." He gave a wry chuckle.

Cam waited a moment for the axe to fall—for Dave to suggest that they call it a night and to take him back home.

But nothing came, and eventually, Cam realized that Dave was waiting for him to reply.

Maybe... maybe he hadn't completely ruined things.

He blew out a breath. "No, no. It's okay. It was sad and hard on the kids, but—" It finally registered then, what Dave had said about him being bi, and Cam shook his head. "It wasn't like I... loved her." He felt it was important to reassure Dave that he wasn't secretly straight. *Oh, the irony.* "What I mean is, I'm not actually attracted to women. At all. We had kids, but I didn't want... I'm not..."

"She didn't know you're gay," Dave finished for him.

Cam nodded, grateful that Dave had rescued him from floundering.

Dave let out a low whistle. "That's pretty intense. I've heard stories like that before, but I've never known anyone who..." He looked at Cam apologetically. "Sorry. I just— Wow. Thirty-five years. You really didn't love her?"

Cam stayed silent, and a moment later, Dave said softly, "I'm usually not this clumsy, I promise. What I meant to say was, it's okay if you did."

Cam didn't know what to do with that. Would it *really* be okay? It was almost unbelievable, the acceptance Dave was giving him. Understanding was a luxury he'd never been exposed to quite enough to know how to handle it.

Dave smacked his hands on his thighs, startling Cam. "Anyway, hey. Let's go in. I've got a reservation for seven thirty."

He opened his door and slid out, and Cam followed suit, reeling from the serious discussion they'd just had. Should they even bother going through with this dinner? He'd never been on a date as an adult before, much less with another guy. This could be nothing more than an exercise in politeness.

He hated thinking of the possibility that this thing with Dave might be over before it even began.

But when they met behind the car, Dave took one look at him and didn't hesitate in wrapping his arms around Cam and pulling him close, a fast, strong embrace of happy reassurance. When he released him a second later, Cam could feel a tentative smile on his face.

"You're an interesting guy, Cam," Dave remarked. "I like interesting."

Cam softened further. "I like you too," he replied, and felt a sharp pang of pride when Dave laughed.

"Come on. Let's eat."

They walked toward the entrance in silence, and Cam allowed himself to hope that maybe, just maybe, being himself wouldn't be so bad after all.

After the initial intensity in Dave's car, they spent dinner discussing much lighter topics. Dave was obviously avoiding asking anything further about LaVerne, and Cam wasn't sure how to feel about that. But he went along with it, not least because he appreciated the effort to keep things comfortable after the more serious turn they'd taken in the car.

The food was excellent, and Cam was glad he'd gone shopping. His navy Dockers would have been out of place at the Cotton Lounge. Dave explained that he'd been at the helm of a couple of software companies that hit pay dirt when they'd been sold off or gone public, and he was now able to have his pick of projects. Cam enjoyed hearing about a world he had little knowledge of and was impressed by Dave's achievements, but what was more amazing was how interesting Dave seemed to find *him*. They talked at length about small-town life, Cam's business, even the future of farming in America.

At one point, Cam asked Dave, "What about you? You know I'm from Bitter, but where are you from?"

Dave looked nonplussed for a moment. "How can we not have talked about that?" He shrugged. "I guess I got distracted. But I grew up in Connecticut."

"Yankee," Cam teased, but it was playful.

Dave's eyes danced in reply. "Yeah, it must be rough for you guys to have me around, reminding you of your inferior baseball teams and questioning the strange need to manufacture everything in the shape of the state of Texas." He snorted. "One of my employees once gave me a miniature bamboo garden that had been forcibly grown to form the outline of Texas."

Cam whooped with laughter. He didn't doubt it was true. Texans loved seeing their beloved state on everything from clothes to cutting boards.

All told, despite the initial awkwardness and Cam's fears that his life had ruined the evening, the date ended up feeling completely normal—and completely wonderful in that normalcy. With every passing minute, Cam found himself growing more attracted to his dinner companion.

At the end of the meal, Dave insisted on paying. "My treat. I invited you out, so I'm paying." He was already sliding his credit card into the leather bill holder. He set the folio on the edge of the table, crossed his arms on the table, and leaned toward Cam. "You can take me out next time."

Next time. He said next time.

Cam was practically dancing in his seat. "I'll do that." He leaned forward too, until their faces were barely a foot apart. "Thank you for dinner. I had a great time."

Dave grinned. "I did too."

The waiter came and took Dave's card, whisking it away and back within a minute. Dave signed the slip and not long after that, the two men were walking out into the crisp night air. They chatted about Texas weather on the drive home, and when Dave pulled into the spot in front of Cam's apartment, he got out of the car, as well.

"I'll walk you up," he told Cam.

The words set Cam's heart into overdrive.

Dave is walking you to your door. Dave might kiss you.

He wanted Dave to kiss him.

He wanted to kiss Dave.

They reached his door too fast. Cam stopped in front of it and turned to Dave. "Do you want to come in?" His voice sounded steady, thank God, even though he could feel his fingers shaking.

Dave gave him a lazy smile. "No, thanks. I mean, I *want* to, but I should get home soon. I have to be up early tomorrow for a conference call."

"Well." Cam drew in an audible breath. *Dang, how embarrassing.* "Thanks again."

And then . . .

Cam saw it almost in slow motion, painfully aware of how desperately he wanted to savor every nuance of this moment. Dave's eyes turning hot and full of intention . . . Cam stepping forward slightly as Dave's head dipped the scant inch that closed the distance between their mouths . . .

Their lips met and sparks exploded in Cam's brain, the feel and smell and sound of Dave's kiss setting off a conflagration like he'd never before experienced. He was reduced to nothing higher than a mass of sensation. Dave's skin was warm, and he tasted of chocolate and wine when his tongue ran lightly over Cam's lips, prompting Cam to open his mouth and allow Dave entrance. The taller man wasted no time in sliding inside, a shallow, sweet lick across Cam's upper palate that had Cam moaning softly.

At the sound, though, Dave began to slowly pull away, the scrape of his slight stubble abrading Cam's cheek in the most delicious, perfect way. Cam wanted to grab him by the lapels and pull him back, to mash their mouths and bodies together until they went up in flames or at least got inside and onto the couch. But Dave was already stepping back, smiling warmly, making Cam feel like he'd actually just *achieved* something much bigger and more glorious than a kiss.

"So. I'll see you Saturday morning?"

Cam heard the real question behind the casual tone. *Are we together now?*

He nodded. "Absolutely."

Dave gave a small wave. "Good night, Cam."

"Good night, Dave," Cam called after Dave, who was already heading back down the stairs from the landing.

His knees felt wobbly, and he shuffled back until he was leaning against the door, forcing himself to take a couple of calming breaths before pushing upright again and turning to unlock the door. He stepped into the apartment, almost wishing he could stay in Austin for good.

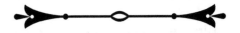

1982

"Did you hear about Roger Henderson?" Bill Garland leaned over the counter with the register, his voice low.

Cam frowned. Roger Henderson had graduated a few years ahead of him and had gone off to college at A&M. He'd come back for the summer before his senior year to help on the Henderson family farm, and Cam had seen him in the shop a couple of times—a short, quiet young man who tended to keep to himself, get his business done, and get out.

Cam frowned. "What about Roger?" He grunted as he lifted a bag of grain back onto the pile from which it had fallen. His feed store had been open a couple of months, and he was working long, grueling hours, trying to get the business to a point where it was viable. He was confident that it would happen over time, since people had been supportive and were more than pleased to be able to have a local place so they didn't have to drive all the way to San Angelo for their feed. But it was a lot of work to get it going, even with the help from his new in-laws.

The few nearby white farmers still seemed to go out of their way to avoid buying from him, but Cam didn't really care. There were enough folks in Bitter and in surrounding towns, and his prices were competitive. He couldn't see their problems causing him any.

They all knew their place, and as long as everyone stayed where they belonged, everything would be fine.

"Doug Hodgkins and his boys beat Roger down last night. His ma found him in the fields this morning. Took him to the hospital in San Angelo."

Beat . . . down . . .

Cam gaped at Bill. "What? Why?"

The heads of the two other customers in the store—Trey Mooney and his brother Marcus, who'd been discussing something about tillers—swiveled toward Cam.

Dang, he'd been too loud.

Cam smiled and nodded at the brothers, acting like everything was just fine. A second later, the two returned to their conversation.

Bill kept his voice low. "Doug saw him at a rest stop on I-10, sitting in a car and muggin' down with a *man*."

The news was delivered with a sneer of disgust, and Cam's blood froze in his veins. He fought the desire to succumb to shock, to crumple to the ground and heave up his breakfast all over the cheap linoleum floor.

He gulped down a few breaths, sure that he looked more than a little strange. But he could always lie and chalk it up to the "unpleasant" idea of two men getting hot and heavy in a tight space.

"Is Sherriff Thomas gonna do anything about it?"

Bill squinted at him. "Why? No one's pressing charges. Roger least of all."

Cam couldn't quite process what he was hearing. "What about Mr. and Mrs. Henderson?"

Bill snorted. "Come off it, Cam. Don't be stupid. Would you raise a ruckus about it, if that were your kid? Embarrassing stuff. They just want it to die down. He's alive, isn't he? That should be enough for them. We all know he won't come back, anyway, and it'll blow over soon enough. Long as the Hendersons don't make trouble about it, I don't see why it has to be an issue."

"Don't make trouble about it"?

Their son had been beaten horribly enough to wind up in the hospital, and Bill was saying it wasn't an issue?

That could have been you.

Cam put his palms down on the counter and pressed hard, trying to find some grounding. "It's a shame," he managed to say. "Roger was always nice to me when we were kids."

Bill huffed. "It's ugly business. He never should have brought that kind of thing to Bitter."

Cam swore he could *feel* his soul curl in on itself. It was a good reminder, but a sobering one too.

As long as everyone stayed where they belonged, everything would be fine.

He gave Bill a tight nod and made a mental note to discount the Hendersons' grain. He couldn't take the risk of visiting Roger in the hospital—people would start seeing that as some kind of a statement, and the hit he'd take to his business would be too great. But at least he could do this small thing to help out the rest of the family. The other kids would be looked upon with suspicion for a while, and Mr. and Mrs. Henderson might be shunned by some of the more conservative folk.

With a sigh, Cam shifted the topic of conversation to the harvest and Bill's sister, who was going to play piano at the upcoming Easter service at church. But thoughts of Roger were never far from his mind the entire time.

That could have been you.

Chapter Six

"Good morning, everyone!"

A smiling, thirtysomething blonde woman had just entered the classroom and greeted the group of six students sitting in the room.

"Welcome to Embroidery for Fun and Relaxation." She beamed at all of them, a motley group comprised of two gray-haired white ladies, a woman who looked in her forties and was wearing a business suit as though she were skipping out on work to indulge in embroidery, two college-aged girls who giggled and inserted the word *totes* into every sentence...

And Cam.

"I'm Jenny Lynn, and I'm really looking forward to spending the next six weeks with all y'all."

Cam could have sworn that sparkles were coming out of her hair, she was so peppy. Jenny Lynn had them go around the room and introduce themselves, telling their name, their *background with embroidery* (was that even a thing?), and why they were in the class. When it finally got around to him, Cam was feeling more than a little self-conscious.

"I'm Cam. I don't have any, uh, embroidery experience." That sounded perverted. "I decided to take this class because I'd never done anything like it before and figured I'd give it a go." *Dang.* Perverted again.

Or maybe he was viewing everything with a sexual lens because, ever since Sunday night, he hadn't been able to get his mind off Dave and that kiss. He'd gone to bed dreaming of it and woken with a near-painful erection.

That morning he'd brought himself to climax to thoughts of someone other than Albert Clark for the first time in his postpubescent life.

"Hi, Cam," chorused the class when he was finished, making him cringe. He probably should have gone for what he'd wanted to do—the creative writing class. But the fear of writing about his own experiences far outweighed the accompanying excitement, so embroidery it was.

Embroidery couldn't possibly cause trouble in his soul like writing might.

"Great! So, we're going to dive right in today with practicing the continental stitch. I have some materials here for all of you." Jenny Lynn handed out pieces of canvas, needles, and some kind of thin yarn. "We're going to practice a little bit with some simple concentric squares."

Jenny Lynn demonstrated, and for a while the entire class was quiet, focusing on their task. After a while, as they all got more comfortable, the group started talking, and Cam learned that Jean and Kate, the gray-haired women, were a couple who wanted to have an activity they could do together; Pratima, the woman in the suit, really *was* on her lunch break—taken extra early, since it wasn't even eleven o'clock in the morning—because she'd been told by her doctor to find a calming hobby to bring down her blood pressure; and the two young women whose names he hadn't quite heard were students at UT who had some free time and felt like learning something frivolous.

Cam stared down at the canvas in his hand, the center covered with a passably good red square.

Was that what he was doing? Killing time with frivolity? Or was it trying to calm himself down before his heart gave out? He wasn't trying to strengthen any relationships through this class.

"What about you, Cam?" One of the young ones—*Maisey?*—asked. "Why did you decide to take this class?"

Cam pulled a newly threaded needle through cloth. He'd chosen brown as his next color, and it didn't show as well alongside the red as he'd hoped. Maybe with more coverage it would look better.

But none of that answered the question he'd been asked.

"I've never done it before," he said, an echo of his little introductory speech.

You wanted to see what you're capable of.

The thought popped up unexpectedly, and he didn't share it. Maybe he was wrong. It seemed like a funny choice of class to test his capabilities.

He looked up then, finding that the other students wore varying degrees of the same look: *typical male answer.*

LaVerne had given him that look at least once a week during their marriage. Patrice nailed him with it every time she saw him. Heck, even Georgia gave him that look.

He froze for a moment.

Georgia was coming to visit in a couple of weeks.

He'd forgotten for a bit, too immersed in the happy surprise that was Dave Montoya.

Well, that would be fine. Dave would understand if Cam needed a little time with his daughter. It wasn't as though they were going to be in each other's pockets within the next couple of weeks, seeing as their next "date" was Saturday. Not even a real date. And Dave had said he was busy with his consulting project, anyway.

There was no reason Georgia had to know. When she went back to Dallas . . .

His secret would stay in Austin where it belonged.

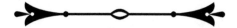

"Hey, handsome."

Dave sauntered over to the table where Cam was sitting in the coffee shop. By this point, Cam considered it "his" table, and a part of him sat there so it would always be easy for Dave to find him.

Like today.

Pedro and Richard had gone to the register to order. Dave put his phone and gloves down at their usual table, pulling his chair closer to Cam's so that they were facing one another at an angle, then sat down, knees bumping up against Cam's thigh. It was so sweet and casually affectionate that Cam couldn't help a pang of regret from squeezing around his heart.

He was going to miss this when he left town.

"Morning, Dave." He smiled wide and reached out a hand to curve around Dave's bare knee, a touch there and gone, but the warmth of Dave's skin, the rough feel of his leg hair beneath Cam's palm, had Cam's body heating fast and furious.

Dave was looking at him with some amusement, as though he knew what Cam was thinking, but there was also desire in his gaze, suggesting that he was thinking the same thing.

Which was . . . what, exactly?

Cam had thought about it far too often this week. He'd imagined himself and Dave, in the positions he'd viewed online. But the reality of sex with another man was causing him both impossible excitement and dread. It was so monumental, this particular unknown, and after more than half a century of life waiting to experience what he so desperately wanted, he wasn't sure he was ready.

"How was your week?" Dave leaned back, putting some space between them, and a second later the other two cyclists showed up holding mugs of coffee. Pedro set one on the table in front of Dave's chair.

Interesting. Dave might be into Cam, but he was cautious with his public affection too—even in front of his friends.

"I started an embroidery class." Cam watched as Dave took in the statement. First surprise, then confusion, followed by amusement, then finally curiosity.

"You're being serious?" Dave asked.

Richard and Pedro had leaned forward, abandoning any pretense of not listening in. It felt good, in a way, to be so easily included in their group.

Cam shrugged. "I was looking for something to do. It's actually fun. Calming."

Pedro barked out a laugh. "I'd stick myself with the damned needle too much for it to be anything close to calming," he observed to the group, and they chuckled at the ridiculous idea of a heart surgeon being clumsy with a needle, before Pedro turned his focus on Cam. "So, are you retired, like our friend here?"

"Which isn't really retirement," Richard cut in.

Cam shook his head. He'd told Dave most of this during their date on Sunday, and even though it still made him feel uncomfortable to share too much with a larger crowd, these guys seemed okay. Friends of Dave and all that.

"I'm just taking a break for a few months."

"A few months' break? Sounds like retirement to me," Richard teased.

"What do you do?" That was Pedro again.

"Grain processing and sales. My business is livestock feed, but my—an employee is running the store for the moment, while I'm away." Given Dave's reaction to the news that Cam had kids, he thought it would be best not to share it with the other guys just yet.

"So you're here for a short time. Then what?" Pedro was full of questions this morning.

"Back to the daily grain grind, I guess." Cam shrugged.

Richard laughed. "I bet you get to use that one a lot."

Cam stole a look at Dave, whose face was surprisingly somber. As he swung his eyes back around to Richard, he noticed that Pedro was also looking at Dave and frowning.

What was that about?

But Cam couldn't ask them in front of Richard. Even in his naiveté about dating, he wasn't completely socially clueless.

He strove to sound normal in his answer to Richard. "Surprisingly, no. Not really. Most guys out my way grew up with that one. Farm life, you know."

Richard leaned back in his chair, seeming to contemplate something, then finally offered, "Well, if you're ever interested in sharing your story more publicly, I think one of my editors would jump at the chance to publish a piece about folks like you."

"Folks like me?" Cam tried to keep the frown off his face.

Richard waved his hand in the air. "Black, born during the Civil Rights movement era, grew up gay in a small religious—I'm assuming religious, anyway, based on the usual profile—farm town . . ."

Richard kept talking, but Cam couldn't hear him past the sudden buzzing in his ears.

Dave held up a hand, and Richard abruptly shut up.

"He's not out yet." Dave said it as though he knew for certain, but when he turned to look at Cam, there was a question in his eyes.

Cam nodded, feeling like he'd just disappointed Dave but not sure how to fix it. But Dave didn't react in any way to his confirmation other than to nod in response.

"Oh, hey. Sorry, Cam." Richard sounded as mortified as Cam felt. "I should have figured that out already. I hope you know I'd never reveal anything about you without your full knowledge and consent."

Cam *didn't* know that, but he believed Richard now. "It's okay."

Dave flashed him a smile and started throwing out alternative topics to pitch to Richard's editors, very obviously working to get the conversation back on track, but everyone seemed to appreciate his efforts. It gave Cam a second to recover, and soon enough he was joining in, as well, offering a few ideas that Richard actually seemed enthusiastic about.

By the time Pedro and Richard left, it was as though the awkward moment had never happened.

At the same time, Cam couldn't help but wonder if he would ever not ruin a conversation with the details of his life. Dave couldn't possibly enjoy dealing with these heavy moments so early on . . . could he?

Speaking of, Dave rotated his chair until he was sitting closer to Cam at the same table. His face looked serious, and Cam started to panic.

Was he about to get dumped?

"Cam," Dave said gently, but there was a solemnity in his voice too. "I need to ask you something."

Cam swallowed hard and nodded for Dave to continue.

"Have you ever been with another man?"

Huh. That was a surprise.

Not a breakup, but not a particularly welcome question, either.

He couldn't really complain, though. Dave had given him nothing but understanding, and refusing to answer seemed almost ungrateful, somehow. Still, it took Cam a second to summon up the courage to reply.

He took a deep breath and forced himself to look Dave in the eye as he spoke. "I was faithful to my wife for all the years we were married." He knew it didn't really answer the question, but he couldn't bring himself to say a simple *No*. He was pretty sure Dave already knew, anyway.

The way Dave's eyes softened made Cam's throat tighten, and he had to pull his gaze away, down toward the table, where he traced a circle over the worn wooden top with his left index finger. "Besides, even if I hadn't been—which was never a question, because I'm not that kind of man—I didn't leave Bitter much. There's no such thing as being gay in my hometown."

"So . . . am I the first man you've kissed?"

Cam froze. Hearing it out loud like that . . .

Was he really that *bad* at it?

Dave must have seen something in Cam's face, because he quickly explained, "I couldn't tell anything from the way you kiss, if that bothers you. I was just thinking about how I hadn't realized until Richard was pressing you for a story that you probably hadn't come out yet. Between that and knowing that your wife died only recently, and you just said you were faithful to her . . ."

Cam swallowed hard and nodded. For some reason, saying, *Yes, you're the first*, was easier than saying, *No, I've never been with a man*.

Yes to Dave. No to some anonymous someone.

"Yeah. You're the first." He averted his eyes. "You probably think I'm a fool."

He let out a tense breath, and silence fell between them as he waited for Dave to end things.

"I think a lot of things about you, but definitely not that you're a fool," Dave told him. "And I understand your situation."

But . . .

Cam waited for the other shoe to drop.

"So we can take things slow. I won't push you into anything before you're ready."

What? Dave wasn't breaking up with him. Yet again, Cam told himself he had to stop thinking in worst-case scenarios, but half a century of fear was making that difficult.

"I don't—"

"I was—"

They both spoke at the same time, then stopped with a self-conscious laugh. Cam waved at Dave. "Go ahead." He wasn't sure what he'd been about to say, anyway.

"Okay." Dave dipped his head so his face was closer to Cam's. "I was wondering if you want to go for a ride with me tomorrow."

Cam could feel the heat rising in his cheeks at the image of Dave riding *him*, and had to clench his hands into fists, fingers biting into the skin of his palm, to keep from moaning too.

Lord, but he was blushing way too frequently these days for his comfort. He uttered a silent prayer of thanks that at least his skin was dark enough that Dave couldn't see it. Dave might have been okay with taking it slow, but apparently Cam's libido wanted to charge full-steam ahead.

"Like, biking, right?" he croaked.

Dave grinned, obviously picking up on where Cam's thoughts had gone. "Yeah, biking."

"I'd really like that, but I don't know if I can keep up," Cam answered honestly. He was in decent shape—strong from years of hauling sacks of feed around and taking long walks all over the countryside—but he hadn't ridden a bike in well over fifteen years, ever since he'd taught the kids how and then promptly put his old Schwinn back in the barn and forgot about it.

Dave laughed. "Not like that. Not what I do with these guys." He gestured toward the empty chairs where Pedro and Richard had been sitting earlier. "I mean, let's take an easy ride around the lake, then we can stop and have a picnic. Relaxed. Slow."

Cam didn't miss the emphasis on that last word. After a lifetime of living a lie, though, even this small step felt like a headlong rush.

But that didn't stop him from saying yes to Dave.

1985

LaVerne held on to Cam's arm as he escorted her up the path leading to the Clarks' front door. He'd tried to convince her to stay home today—it had been less than a day since she'd miscarried their first pregnancy and she was exhausted from the cramps and blood loss—but she'd insisted on coming.

It felt wrong.

All of it.

Given that they'd been married for four years and she hadn't gotten pregnant in that time, he'd almost convinced himself that it simply wasn't going to happen. That belief had lulled him into a sense of relief, because he adhered to the commonly held belief that men who liked men shouldn't be fathers. He'd never questioned it. Simply accepted that some higher power had made the correct decision for him, and gone on with life.

But he hadn't taken into account the fact that he and LaVerne weren't intimate with anything approaching significant frequency, and the chances of pregnancy when sex happened sporadically at best weren't always high.

Still, when she'd told him three weeks ago that she was a month along, he'd been shocked. Angry. Scared.

By yesterday afternoon, though, when she'd called him up at the store, sobbing and barely coherent, to tell him that she'd lost the baby, the news had hit him hard in a way he hadn't thought would matter. He'd spent the day torn between comforting LaVerne and dealing with the revelation that he'd never *truly* accepted, in his heart of hearts, that he might not have children in his lifetime. That, actually, he wanted them and felt that he deserved a chance to be a father.

If only.

It didn't matter now, anyway.

They were several feet from the door. Cam slowed. "Are you sure you don't need to be resting at home, LaVerne? You look drawn."

She stiffened, and he could tell he'd made her angry, but she relaxed quickly and turned to look up at him. "I know you're worried. I appreciate that, but I want to be here. It's not every day that one of my friends graduates college."

Beneath the exhaustion, he heard something else in her voice. Almost like . . . longing.

It made him wonder.

"Do you—do you ever think about it? Going to college?"

It wasn't the question to ask in this moment, standing exhausted a few steps away from what was supposed to be a happy celebration of someone else's achievements, but Cam couldn't resist. He had been with LaVerne for six years, but he'd never considered that she might want to do something like that. He'd assumed they were both destined to live unremarkable lives in Bitter, because that's what they'd both been raised to know. Even Sandra, who had her college degree, was moving back home to work here and live out her days in Bitter.

This was their place in the world. The community of Bitter didn't just provide protection from the hurts and prejudices of the outside world; it was a source of pride for its residents. They'd built it together. They all owned it. Something like that wasn't an easy thing to leave behind.

A soft sigh preceded her words, and he felt her lean into him, ever so slightly. "I'd love to. I want to be in education administration. Not just teaching. I know I could do something good for the schools here that goes beyond day-to-day classroom work. I think sometimes about taking correspondence courses or even registering for a class in San Angelo. It's not too bad a drive if I only do it once or twice a week." She looked into the distance. "I could learn how to drive."

LaVerne wanted to drive too?

A car pulled up, reminding Cam that they needed to get moving before folks started nosing around, wondering what was wrong. He used the car's arrival as an excuse to buy more time, though, turning under the pretense of waiting for whomever had come before going inside.

"You could go," he said under his breath, watching as Tillie and Darnell Booker got out of their new sedan.

Darnell waved. Cam lifted a hand in reply as LaVerne let out a quiet snort.

"Me, go to college?"

Well, now she sounded like she didn't want to go. It didn't make sense. He worked to keep the frown off his face. Tillie and Darnell were heading up the walk toward them. "Why not?" he murmured.

Out of the corner of his eye, he saw LaVerne twist around to look up at him.

"You're serious."

He gave a small nod.

"I—" LaVerne began, but that was as far as she got before Tillie and Darnell were upon them, shaking hands (the men), sharing hugs (the women), and everyone exclaiming over Sandra Clark's accomplishment.

They went into the house and, a minute later, were standing in a small circle around the woman of honor, hearing about her graduation ceremony and plans for her future. Cam was trying to listen, but his mind was replaying the conversation he'd had with LaVerne just before they'd been interrupted. If LaVerne did take him up on his oddly impulsive offer, that would probably mean postponing having children for a few more years. That might earn him a reprieve from sex with his wife, but having recently discovered his desire for children, he felt it as much a loss as a boon.

No decisions have been made yet, remember. You don't even know what she'd been about to say.

He told himself to wait until he had a chance to talk to LaVerne, but it wasn't helping that Sandra started reminiscing about the dorm she'd lived in, campus life, and final exams. He could see how enthralled LaVerne was by every little detail.

Unfortunately, his distraction put him in a more vulnerable position than he was used to. He smelled the cologne a split second before Albert Clark clapped him on the back, pulling Cam close for a side hug while shouting, "That's my little sister!"

The feel of Albert's warm, firm body against his, even if it was only hip to hip and shoulder to shoulder, had Cam moaning out loud.

Albert jerked away from him as though Cam had just spit fire, and stared with a look of confusion, horror, and shock all mixed together.

The entire group was looking in puzzlement at the exchange. Had they heard Cam moan like that too? Goodness, they probably had.

Think. Think. Think.

Cam immediately twisted his face into a grimace and brought one hand up to rub his shoulder before relaxing his features into what he hoped was an apologetic expression. "Hey, Albert. Didn't mean to alarm you. Shoulder's a bit sore. I lifted a feed sack wrong yesterday and it really tightened up in the night."

The stark relief on Albert's face was like a knife to the chest.

"You didn't tell me that," LaVerne's gentle chide reached his ears.

"I didn't want to worry you," he said softly, trying not to make the lie too loud, as if the volume of it affected his chances of going to Hell.

But everyone else must have viewed it as a romantic admission, because there was a collective sigh from the women before Darnell snorted and said, "Hey, thanks, McGhee. Now Tillie's gonna be all over me about how I'm not as sappy as you."

Wrong, wrong, wrong.

Everything was wrong.

But Cam did what he usually did, which was to smile, nod, and go along with it. Thankfully, the group drifted apart shortly after that, and Cam found himself by the sideboard, which was covered in dishes heaped high with food. He was loading up a plate when Mrs. Henderson walked up, looking over the offerings with small sounds of praise.

She and Cam greeted one another, and she gestured to the crowd that had shown up for the party. "It's just so heartwarming to see how much everyone in this town supports education. I feel just as proud as if she were my own daughter, you know. A child from Bitter with a college degree is something to celebrate, indeed. My own Jonah will graduate next year and you can rest assured we'll be calling on the whole town to join us in a gathering like this too."

Cam's fingers were gripping his plate too tight.

Mrs. Henderson was the mother of Roger Henderson, the young man who'd been so severely beaten for getting caught kissing another man. Last Cam had heard, he'd recovered enough to go back to school and had graduated college at the end of that school year.

Two years ago.

There had been no announcement for Roger. No party. When Cam had seen Mr. Henderson in the store the summer following what would have been Roger's graduation, he'd asked about the ceremony.

Mr. Henderson's mouth had gone tight, his lips set in a grim line, before he'd told Cam, "We don't recognize that name in our lives any longer."

Cam had been taken aback. The Hendersons hadn't been too open when Roger had ended up in the hospital, and Roger hadn't set foot back in Bitter since that night, but Cam hadn't realized they'd disowned their son entirely.

Hearing Mrs. Henderson gush about Jonah now as though *he* would be the first of their children to graduate college . . .

It wasn't fair. It would never be fair.

When they left the party, LaVerne told him in the truck on the way home that, yes, she wanted to learn to drive, and she wanted to go to college. After everything that had happened that day, he didn't even think twice before answering, "If that's what you want, you should have it. No one should be denied their dreams, LaVerne. *No one.*"

She reached out and set a small, gentle hand on his shoulder. "Thank you, Cam." Her fingers massaged his muscles.

"I'm glad your shoulder is feeling better," she added, and the tone of her voice put Cam on alert. He belatedly realized she was rubbing the very shoulder he'd said he'd hurt, and he hadn't so much as flinched.

She knows I lied.

Did she know why?

"You're a good man. The best husband a girl could ask for."

But it sounded like she was saying it more to convince herself than to compliment him.

They drove the rest of the way home in silence.

Chapter Seven

Cam pulled into the driveway of a stunningly beautiful home in Westlake. Built of limestone with a terracotta roof, the house stood nearly three stories high at the top of a long, circular driveway.

He felt all too aware of his battered truck as he parked it next to the three-car garage. When Dave had given Cam the address so they could meet here this morning and make sure Cam had a bike that fit him properly, it didn't occur to Cam that Dave might live in what would easily be considered a mansion if it had been located back in Bitter.

Heck. It was a mansion no matter where it was. The only difference was that this neighborhood was full of them. As he'd driven up the hill that Dave's street was on, he'd passed several enormous places, each one custom designed and immaculately kept. It was like he'd fallen into a movie set.

He shut off the engine and hopped out of the truck to head to the front door, which was set back beneath a large stone archway. He was reaching for the doorbell when the heavy, carved wooden door swung open, revealing Dave in a pair of loose chinos and a light sweater, looking utterly delicious.

All thoughts of inadequacy fell away as Dave stepped forward with a quiet "Hi, Cam," and kissed him.

It was just like last time.

Except more.

Better.

Cam didn't hesitate this time to open his mouth, letting Dave inside on a soft groan. He brought his hands up to Dave's shoulders, reveling in the firm curves of muscle, sliding his right palm up to feel the strong cords of Dave's neck.

Dave's hands were moving too, wrapping around Cam's back and slowly pulling him forward, mouths melding as their bodies grew closer.

Their hips met, and even through the thick fabric of his jeans, Cam felt the unmistakable solid ridge of Dave's erection, and the resulting tide of violent *need* had him yanking his mouth away, ripping himself from Dave's arms and staggering back a few steps.

His body was heaving, breaths coming hard and fast, and he could barely see past the blurry spots of light that had crept into his vision.

"Cam?" Dave didn't move, but Cam could hear the panting desire in Dave's voice underlaced with concern and confusion.

"Was too good," he managed to grunt out. "Too . . ." Speaking was helping his body to calm down, but apparently his mind was still struggling to catch up. He took a deep breath and straightened.

He wanted the ground to open up and swallow him. Why did he have to ruin *everything* with his inexperience?

"I feel the same way." Dave let out a self-deprecating laugh. "But I told you we'd take things slow, and it looks like I forgot my promise already." He held out a hand. "Shall we go inside? I'll finish packing up lunch, and we can head out."

Calm down. He's not kicking you out.

Being with Dave might feel natural, but it definitely wasn't *easy.*

Cam managed to pull himself together, then slipped his hand into Dave's and smiled. "Sounds great." He allowed Dave to lead him forward, and just before they entered the house, he commented, "You have a beautiful home."

The remark was so banal, one uttered so commonly out of obligation, that both men recognized how absurd it sounded after such an intense embrace. Cam immediately began to laugh at himself, and Dave followed suit. It occurred to Cam, as they stepped over the threshold and he took in the gorgeous open room whose wall-to-wall windows on the opposite side revealed an incredible view over the hills, that if he were a braver person—a better person—who didn't care so much about keeping this part of his life contained in Austin, he could make a *life* with Dave. The possibility of *easy* was suddenly, tantalizingly within reach.

In the next second, though, he thought of Elijah and Georgia and brushed the thought away before following Dave into the kitchen.

The ride around the park was exactly as Dave had promised. Easy and slow, meandering around the trails while they talked. Dave explained that the park trails went farther, into an area called the Greenbelt, where Cam might be interested in hiking, but for their ride, they stayed mostly on paved paths.

They rolled along at a sedate pace until they came to a wide, grassy expanse, where they stopped and walked their bikes to a spot in the middle of the rolling lawn. From where they stood, they could see the buildings of downtown, gleaming in the bright early-March sunshine. The weather had chilled once more, but Cam was comfortable in his hoodie and long-sleeved T-shirt.

Dave opened up one of the bags hanging from a rack behind the seat of his bike and pulled out a rolled-up blanket, spreading it out onto the grass, then went back to the pannier and pulled out a wrapped box. He set the box on the edge of the blanket, then they both sat, side by side, facing the skyline.

Amazing.

Cam took in the view and felt himself relaxing by degrees. Dave's fingers moved over his, coming to rest atop Cam's hand, and Cam could swear he *felt* something deep inside of him begin to unwind.

He couldn't resist leaning over and pressing his lips to Dave's, feeling a swell of pride that he'd been the one to instigate this time. The kiss was soft and sweet, so different from the one they'd shared earlier that morning, but there was still the hot, simmering attraction just beneath the surface, and when he drew away, he was elated to find Dave looking heavy-lidded and liquid-boned.

I did that. I made a man feel like that.

Cam had to turn away to keep from kissing Dave again. He couldn't get so caught up that they risked behaving too audaciously in a public place.

"Do you, uh, come here often?" he asked, taking a deep breath of fresh, cool air.

Dave made a low humming noise that shot up Cam's spine like an electric caress.

"Not really. I think about it because I tell myself I should take it easy more often and I don't need to work myself so hard anymore, but saying and doing are two very different things."

Cam understood completely. He kept telling himself that he was here for a short time to explore, but it was easier said than done. But he wasn't ready to talk about it yet. Maybe he never would be. He didn't think Dave would take it well, anyway, if Cam came right out and announced that whatever was just beginning between them could only be temporary.

Dave had to know, anyway.

Right?

Cam looked over at Dave, who was now leaning back, basking in the sunlight, tanned skin glowing gold.

Gorgeous.

"I still don't really understand what you did—*do*—for work. You were the CEO of an IT company, but I can't picture that being a consulting position. It sounds like you're doing something more hands-on now."

Dave laughed. "Are you implying that I haven't actually retired? I see Pedro has influenced you already." He shrugged, his grin dropping a bit. "You're right, I don't do executive-level stuff. Not that I'd want to, either. I got tired of the dog and pony show that comes with being at the top, to be honest. Now I work with junior-level managers, coaching them on everything from product design to personnel issues. I wanted to go back to doing something I actually enjoyed, and I'm lucky enough to be able to do it."

Cam huffed. "I'm impressed. You clearly did well for yourself, and it's admirable that you decided to scale it back for the sake of your happiness."

Dave was quiet, looking at Cam with a serious expression, and Cam inwardly cringed.

"For the sake of your happiness."

He felt too exposed.

But Dave didn't take advantage of the opportunity to turn the focus to Cam's romantic regrets. "Sounds to me that your professional track was pretty similar."

Cam barked out a laugh and shook his head. "Nothing like your level." He thought of the dingy carpet and secondhand, worn-out furniture in his rented apartment. On a scale of zero to posh, it wasn't that much different from his place at home, while Dave lived in a near-palace.

Dave slipped his hand over Cam's and rested it there, warm, calloused skin on the back of Cam's hand. "No, I think it's pretty similar. We're both self-made men, Cam, who needed to get away from the demands of routine and make sure we don't waste the rest of our lives through obligations and other people's expectations. Maybe that's why I like you so much." He shrugged. "Either way, I find this time of my life a nice change of pace from the decades I spent with people wanting to ride on the back of my success. In being selfish, I've also found a lot more patience and peace to give to others."

Cam was quiet for a minute, savoring the feel of Dave's closeness. Finally, he nodded slowly. "Can't say I quite experienced it *exactly* that way, but yes, I know what you mean. It's good to have a break and not to feel like I'm just a stand-in for someone else's needs. And I was tired of being used for my accomplishments. A few of the boys I grew up with are always hanging around, still trying to get discounts on their feed just because we knew each other way back when."

Dave's mouth quirked as though he was holding back a laugh.

"Go on and laugh." Cam smiled at him. "I'm sure it's funny to city folk. Where I'm from, we see all the high-powered stuff on TV, but life in the sticks probably feels like living in another universe to y'all."

Dave let out a loud guffaw. "I'm sorry. I really am."

Cam grinned. "That sounds very sincere."

When Dave's laughter finally died down, he asked, "So you said last time that you walk a lot?"

"Yeah, I got to know the city the first week by walking around it, but it's hard to be out and about on the pavement for so many hours. I'm used to fields and dirt roads."

"How many is 'many hours'?"

"About four. Sometimes five."

Dave's jaw dropped. "You wandered the city for that long each day? And for several days running, I assume?"

Cam nodded. "I like walking. I still do it every day, just not for as long. I've found a few nice nature places that work, but it's not the same. That's probably one of the few things I miss. And out west, it's easier to get out of my head in the quiet. Sometimes we'd drive out to El Paso or New Mexico and camp, hike, that kind of thing. There, the quiet is beautiful. My kids love being out that way too. But it's been a long time since we last camped. We had to give it up when my wi—"

Cam stopped with a shake of his head. "Well, maybe I'll go again next year."

Dave gave him a curious look. "Hey, Cam . . . if I'm right—and I really think I'm right—you were about to say something about your late wife. Why did you stop?"

Of course Dave would have noticed. Cam had been too careless about it. He'd gotten carried away, feeling so comfortable talking to Dave that he'd forgotten.

He picked at a blade of grass. "It feels wrong, somehow. Like if I let that part of my life mix with this part, I'll have to acknowledge that somewhere along the way, I messed up. That I'm hurting one or the other somehow."

Dave nodded. "I see."

"You do?"

Dave laughed. "Not really. But yeah." He shrugged. "I mean, I don't really know what it's like, because I was lucky enough not to have to maintain two separate selves. But it's important to you, so . . . I see."

"Thank you."

Dave changed the subject then, asking Cam more about his business, and Cam found a pleasant comfort in being able to describe the process of taking in grain, mixing or processing it into different kinds of animal feed, and some of the machinery that existed for bagging, weighing, and transporting all the moving parts.

They somehow moved on to discussing reality TV, and somewhere in there Dave opened up the sandwiches he'd packed and they ate a leisurely meal under a blue sky.

By the time they packed up and started back, it was well into the afternoon, and they were both content to ride to Dave's SUV in companionable silence.

When they arrived at the house and Dave invited Cam inside, Cam declined.

"I better get going, actually."

He didn't have anything specific to do back home, but the kids usually called on Sunday, and Cam felt bad for not being home for such a long stretch of time. He was getting eager to call them and check in, but he didn't want to do it from Dave's. Georgia for certain would ask too many questions about whose number was showing up on her caller ID.

Maybe he should consider getting a cell phone, after all.

They were standing in front of the driver's-side door of Cam's truck, saying good-bye. "I had a really good time today, Cam," Dave murmured, stepping close. "Want to come over on Wednesday? We can order in, watch a movie. Just kick back."

He kissed Cam. Quick and with intention, before Cam could even answer.

When he did speak, he was already breathless. "Yeah. I'd like that."

Alone in Dave's house. No prying eyes, no image to protect or uphold...

His breath quickened even more.

"Great." Dave dropped another of those rough, fast kisses on his mouth. "I'll see you then."

Cam was the one to lean in this time, first caressing Dave's mouth with his, then pushing his tongue past Dave's lips to rub over the other man's teeth, grunting at the pressure of Dave's lower body against his. His mind was flooded with images of Dave naked, touching Cam's body, offering his hard shaft to Cam's mouth, cords of his arms tightening as he plunged into—

"You should go." Dave had ripped his mouth away from Cam's and was growling, lips curled back from his teeth like a feral animal.

Cam fought the perverse desire to refuse, to stand his ground and see what would happen. But Dave was right. Cam wasn't ready for this, despite his racing imagination.

He should go.

Groping behind himself for the door handle, he found it with unsteady fingers, wrenched open the door, and backed into the car, keeping his eyes on Dave's the entire time, like a stare down between two wild animals.

The sound of the door slamming shut, putting a thick sheet of metal between their bodies, seemed to snap them both out of the lust-fueled trance they'd been caught in.

Cam started the engine, rolled down the window, and lifted a hand. "I'll see you Wednesday."

"Bye, Cam." Dave waved, then slid his hands into his trouser pockets and rocked back on his heels, watching as Cam reversed into the circular drive and headed out, off the property. In the rearview mirror, he could see Dave standing there, staring at the truck even as it turned onto the main street and disappeared from sight.

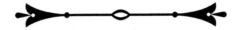

1990

She'd done it.

Cam stood and cheered when LaVerne walked across the stage at Angelo State University's commencement. Mr. and Mrs. Russo sat on his right side, and Mom sat on the other, smiling and clapping along with the crowd as LaVerne accepted her diploma.

He sat back down and reached over to squeeze Mom's hand, happy that she'd come out this afternoon. Since Dad had suffered a stroke last year and was now confined to a wheelchair, Mom had been struggling. She spent all her time caring for him and had withdrawn from a lot of her social activities as a result. Some days, Cam would stop by the house to find that Mom hadn't showered in days. Despite his compromised ability to speak, Dad had been able to communicate, through slurred words and angry, shaky movements, his frustration with Mom's unwillingness to care for herself.

But Cam hadn't been able to convince her to do it, either. He'd suggested a simple medical checkup to start with, hoping the doctor might be able to urge Mom to action, to no avail. He'd tried to get his older sisters to persuade Mom to have her health evaluated, but even the combined efforts of all four of them hadn't succeeded.

He was worried about both of his parents, and on top of all that, Mom wouldn't stop going on about how Dad was destined to die without seeing a grandchild from his only son. It didn't seem to register with her that they already had thirteen grandchildren from her other children. She hadn't let up on Cam about having children of his own, and at times her complaints had spilled over to criticism of LaVerne's pursuit of her degree.

Thank goodness his older sister Carol had agreed to stay with Dad today so Mom could come with Cam and the Russos to LaVerne's graduation. It seemed to be exactly the motivation Mom had needed to put on something pretty, make up her face, and smile for the first time in too long.

And today, so far she'd had nothing but positive comments about LaVerne's accomplishments, and no remarks about their potential for becoming parents.

She clapped and smiled, and after the ceremony, when they met LaVerne in the big auditorium with flowers, hugs, and words of praise, Mom gave LaVerne a long hug. "I feel the pride not just of a mother, but of a fellow woman to be able to say that my daughter-in-law is a *college graduate*," she told LaVerne, who beamed.

Cam felt a swell of love for his mother in that moment, for putting aside her own desires to give this day fully over to another person's accomplishments.

They all went out for dinner afterward, and again Mom made a point to tell LaVerne how proud she was, congratulated Mr. and Mrs. Russo again, and when they went their separate ways, hugged and kissed Cam good night. He and LaVerne were going to stay in a hotel in San Angelo for the night to commemorate LaVerne's graduation, while Mom headed back to Bitter with the Russos.

Cam did his duty that night, eyes shut tight in the dark hotel room, conjuring up the imaginary but reliable version of a naked, muscled, aroused Albert Clark beneath him as he thrust into his wife.

"Oh, Cam," LaVerne sighed after he'd rolled off her and lay in silence as he worked through the disjointed, angry self-loathing that always followed. "This is the happiest day of my life."

But the happiness didn't last.

The hotel room phone rang at four in the morning with the news that Cam's father had passed away in the night. Mom had gotten home late and gone to sleep in the guest bedroom so that she wouldn't wake her husband or Carol, who had fallen asleep in the big armchair next to Dad's side of the bed. When Carol had snapped awake at half past three, her cries of anguish upon finding Dad's cooling body had awoken Mom, who'd come running.

Carol told Cam later that she'd never seen their mother look as young and refreshed as she had in the moment when she realized Dad was gone.

When Elijah John McGhee was laid to rest beneath a whitewashed cross in the Bitter Presbyterian Cemetery, Cam inherited the family farm and the big white farmhouse where he'd grown up, anchoring him that much deeper to an eternity in Bitter.

Chapter Eight

"Dad! I tried to call you three times today. Where have you been? I was worried about you."

Cam rolled his eyes, but it made him laugh to realize how much he was acting like Georgia when she'd been a teenager, and she was behaving like LaVerne used to, fretting and scolding out of love.

"Hi, Georgia." Cam stretched the phone cord taut so he could sit down in one of the dining table chairs while he talked to her. "I was out. How've you been, honey?"

"Where were you?" she demanded.

Lord, but that girl was like a dog with a bone.

"I went to the park. Wanted to get to know the city a little better and be outside," he explained, hoping it would be enough to appease her curiosity. He didn't want to mention Dave.

"Oh." Georgia sounded suddenly deflated. "Was it nice?"

Cam felt a pang of guilt over hurting her. "It was. Maybe I should get a cell phone, though."

That did the trick. Perked her up and switched the subject. "You should! I could help you pick one out when I'm down there next week. I'm going to drive down on Saturday, okay? I'll probably arrive in the afternoon and we can go phone shopping then. You could even get your own email account once you have a phone!"

Cam screwed up his face in distaste. Email. He had an account for the store, but he only ever checked it when he was there. Elijah had the password now and managed all of that correspondence from the old desktop computer in Cam's office.

Then again, Elijah had been prodding Cam to update everything for the business, from the way they tracked their inventory to the signage for all the goods and the warehouse. Cam had given his son the green light, not really because he thought he needed all that stuff, but to give Elijah a chance to direct his energy into something that would be good for his future. The Air Force Academy had given his son a top-rate education in information systems and then helped him apply all that knowledge in the four years after graduation during which Elijah had served as an officer.

Now, he had left the military and was champing at the bit to continue his career growth, but Bitter didn't exactly offer a wealth of opportunities when it came to professional development.

Cam still couldn't quite come to terms with the fact that Elijah had come back to Bitter. Of course, everyone did. They all returned—wasn't that his earliest memory, that Bitter was where he belonged?—but for some reason Elijah's choice had thrown Cam for a loop and he hadn't been able to get over it just yet.

On the other hand, the timing couldn't have been better, since Elijah had come home in time to fill in for Cam while he was in Austin. But the opportunity for growth and change and Elijah's future . . . well, that still had to be created.

"Yeah," he told Georgia. "I could do that."

I could create that opportunity for myself.

They chatted about plans for her visit. Cam's thoughts kept straying to Dave. He wished he could introduce Dave to Georgia, but . . .

But what?

Do you think she would tattle on you?

No. She would understand what was at stake. The business back home. The regard and acceptance of their longtime friends in Bitter. She wouldn't say anything.

He didn't think so, anyway. But it would hurt her. It would open up a lot of questions and pain that Cam didn't think she was ready for.

You mean that you're *not ready for.*

"Dad? Are you still there?" Georgia's voice sounded sharp through the phone.

"Oh, uh, yeah. Sorry, honey. I got distracted by . . . something."

Georgia huffed. "Honestly, you and Elijah both are so bad at talking on the phone."

Thank goodness she chalked it up to a general personality trait rather than pressing him about what had distracted him.

"Anyway, I love you. I'll let you go since you've reached your limit of phone time," Georgia teased. "But I'll see you Saturday, okay? I'm excited to spend a week with you in Austin. It's gonna be so much fun!"

They said their good-byes and hung up, and it dawned on Cam that Georgia's visit meant a week without seeing Dave.

He sighed. This was starting to get more complicated than he'd expected when he'd first moved to Austin. He wasn't sure how to handle it, but he knew one thing: at the end of these few months when he had to return to Bitter, letting Dave go was going to hurt more than anything Cam had ever experienced.

An opportunity lost.

"Good morning, everyone!"

Jenny Lynn swished into the classroom that Tuesday morning wearing a 1950s-style dress and a sweater with a patch sewn onto it that said *Badass Bitch.*

She was an odd little bottle-blonde white lady, and Cam found himself liking her. Everyone except Cam *oohed* and *ahhed* over her patch, and she clearly basked in the compliments. For his part, Cam commented that it looked very professional.

Jenny Lynn beamed. "I'm so glad y'all like it! I wore it because it's an example of what we'll be doing in class today."

Cam raised a brow. He was *not* going to embroider *Badass Bitch* on his sweater no matter how much he liked Jenny Lynn as a teacher.

She clapped her hands together. "Today we'll focus on creating curves with our stitches. Cursive words are a really fun and interesting way to practice making smooth curves. So that's what I'm asking all y'all to do. Think of a word, maybe two, that you want to embroidery. If you need ideas, maybe it's something that describes you, or you can use one of your hobbies or the name of someone you love, like a kid or a pet . . . whatever you'd like. But ideally it will be personal."

Cam was nonplussed. A *personal* word?

Man. Black. Cam. Father. Gay. Widower. Businessman. Explorer. Afraid.

He blinked at his train of thought.

"These will make beautiful framed artwork for your home or, if you sew, you can even put them on an article of clothing for all the world to see!"

Calm down, Jenny Lynn.

Perhaps he should choose something more generic.

"While you're thinking of your words, I'll show you the stitches, and we can start designing," Jenny Lynn announced.

He could just use his name. *Cam.* That was nice and round. Short, too.

You know what other name would look good on your clothes? Dave.

Lord, he was in a choice mood today.

Jenny Lynn spent a few minutes showing them the stitches. Cam struggled to focus, but managed to get into the lesson enough to at least get the basics down.

Once she'd finished demonstrating, Jenny Lynn gave them a few minutes to work on their designs.

"What did you choose, Maisey?" Jenny Lynn strolled over to where one of the college girls was busy penciling something onto a piece of canvas.

Maisey practically bubbled out of her chair. "I'm doing *Happy!*" And then her mood became completely serious before she added, "Because I'm a happy person."

Cam would have laughed if her earnestly clueless demeanor didn't remind him of Georgia.

Man, he'd grown old. Somewhere along the way, he'd reached a point where he didn't want to go back to the low-level dimensions of his youth. Despite the aches and pains of his aging body, he'd been through too much—learned too much—to give it all up for a few looser muscles.

Jenny Lynn smiled. "That's wonderful. Great design. You could add some confetti or flowers around it if you wanted to highlight the word even more."

He noticed that even Jenny Lynn's enthusiasm had been tempered in the face of such unbridled sunshine. It was as though the innocent happiness was reminding all the older people in the class how good they had it.

If that's truly what you believe, why not tell Georgia the truth when she comes to visit?

It was strange reasoning, but the thought was there. He tried to untangle it with his conscious mind, but all he ended up with were the arguments *against* telling her.

Afraid.

"Anyone else?" Jenny Lynn called out.

"I chose *Survivor*," Jean spoke up, then took in a breath and smoothed her hand over the fabric rectangle. "Because I've survived . . . a lot."

There was a story there. Of course there was. Jean's face, so solemn and wistful, was enough of a testament to hardships unspoken. Everyone saw how Kate reached out and took Jean's hand, and the two shared a look of such unconditional love and support that it made Cam's teeth grit against the desire to scream. Not to shout any words or direct it at anyone but the air. Just . . . *scream.*

And here he'd thought it would be the writing class that would push him to get too personal, too fast. But he'd had to make a choice with the knowledge and assumptions he'd had on hand, and even with the way this particular class was making him feel today, he still didn't believe he'd chosen wrong.

Not like the rest of his life.

And just like that, it came to him.

He grabbed up his scrap of fabric and began to trace the outline of his word.

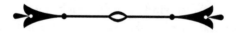

1991

"Cam?" LaVerne looked at him from across the table.

She'd gotten a job in the county school district administration office, which meant she had to commute an hour each way to work every day. At least the work day ended along with the elementary schools, so she was usually able to get home by five o'clock.

Today, though, she'd come home from work barely half an hour ago—well after six o'clock, looking haggard.

By now, he was used to being the one to get dinner on the table and clean up the dishes so she could get some much-needed sleep. Her weak constitution was simply a part of life at this point.

He scooped up a forkful of potatoes, glancing at her briefly in recognition. "Yep?"

"I'm pregnant," she blurted.

Cam's fork clattered onto his plate, food spraying onto the tablecloth, but LaVerne was already talking over the commotion, probably having anticipated this reaction.

"I'm ten weeks along. I'm not running around on you, in case you were worried. I didn't tell you right away this time, though, in case I lost the baby again. That's all. I didn't want to get your hopes up, like last time."

Ten weeks. They hadn't had sex in over a month, which on the one hand suited Cam just fine, but on the other, he *had* been alarmed for a moment there that she might be seeing someone else.

And then the rest of what she said sank in. She'd noticed how he'd felt last time they'd gone through a pregnancy. Six years and there hadn't been another one until now—she'd been in school and neither had felt particularly amorous most of the time—but of course she remembered his disappointment over the miscarriage.

He reached over the table to take her hand. "Hey, Vernie. You could have—you *should* have told me. This is great news. Have you seen the doctor yet?"

He winced at the question. If there was any need for evidence that they were living essentially separate lives, that question would certainly serve. What kind of man didn't know when his wife was pregnant and whether she was getting medical care for their unborn child? Existing side by side, rather than diving into a deeper partnership, was a choice they hadn't consciously made, but he'd attributed it to their busy schedules, LaVerne's tendency to exhaustion, and his preference for—

He coughed, pushing the thought out of his mind. He'd managed in the past couple of years to reach a point where he could almost forget about his desires. Even Albert Clark hadn't made as frequent an appearance in his daydreams now that Cam was working harder to consciously block those sorts of fantasies.

"I haven't yet." She twisted her mouth in an apologetic grimace. "I know it's silly and superstitious, but I felt like it would be bad luck."

Cam felt himself growing angry. She'd put the health of their unborn child, her own health too, at risk out of ignorance. She was college educated. More academically accomplished than he was. She should know better than that.

When this baby was born, Cam would make sure that his child was learned. This kid would speak out against ignorance. Son or daughter, the next generation of McGhees would do the right thing and—

Like you spoke out against the mistreatment of Roger Henderson? Like you did the right thing and worked to educate people that gay doesn't mean bad?

Cam's anger deflated immediately.

He shook his head and squeezed her hand once in reassurance. "I understand why you didn't go."

"So . . . you're not mad?" Her voice was kind of wobbly.

He got up and went to stand near her chair, draping an arm around her. He might not want her sexually, but that didn't mean he didn't care for her as a friend, and he could see how afraid and hurt she was. "No, I'm not mad."

It was the truth. His anger at *her* was gone, anyway. The lingering sense of general injustice felt a lot like anger, but he didn't think it was relevant. She didn't need to know. She *couldn't* know, because then he'd have to explain why it was so strong. So personal.

"Are you happy about the baby?" She looked up at him, eyes pleading.

He nodded. "I am." Even he could tell that his voice rang with conviction. He *wanted* to be a father. He wanted the chance to influence a child who would do better than Cam had done.

LaVerne started to cry—whether from happiness, relief, or simple hormones, Cam couldn't tell, but he responded by bending down, scooping her out of her chair, and taking her to the couch to cradle and soothe her until she fell asleep.

Elijah Roger McGhee was born six months later, surprising Cam and LaVerne by coming earlier and faster than expected in the middle of the night. Cam held the infant in the darkness as LaVerne recovered from the draining birth. He stroked Elijah's soft hair and tiny hands while he thought about the lessons he wanted to teach his son.

Be yourself seemed . . . hypocritical. At best.

Be kind was a given, and yet Cam had seen how it was reserved only for those of whom the rest of Bitter approved. Even sons weren't exempt from disapproval that could cost a man a lifetime of love.

It didn't stop him from wanting to see those things in his child, though. He wanted to be able to point to something in his life and say, *This is the good I gave to the world.*

He'd done so many things wrong, while this little boy, Elijah, felt like absolution in his first few minutes of life. Forgiveness for the multitude of sins Cam had perpetrated against his friends, his wife . . . himself.

Be forgiving.

He could teach that, at the least. Forgiveness. And perhaps, in the end, that was all anyone ever needed.

Chapter Nine

Dave opened the door upon Cam's ring and smiled. "Hey, handsome."

A handful of hours they'd spent in one another's company and already Dave had an effect on Cam that was unlike anything else he'd ever experienced. Seeing Dave relaxed Cam. Talking to Dave made Cam feel as though he was capable of anything. Kissing Dave made Cam feel . . .

Whole.

Right.

So right that Cam had already spent too much energy on *not* thinking about how little time he had left with this man. And yet, thirty seconds in Dave's company and already wild, foolish thoughts were taking over. Little snippets of what life could be like if Cam simply chose to stay in Austin. Happy, joyous possibilities.

Except it wasn't that simple.

"Hey, yourself." Cam paused just inside the entryway to kiss Dave hello. The now-familiar excitement he felt at being lips to lips with a sexy man like Dave was making him feel jangled up. Ready.

For what, though, he wasn't quite sure.

When they broke apart, Dave's eyes were full of heat. "Hungry?" he murmured, and Cam felt something electric spark through his body.

This is what it's supposed to feel like.

Dave swung the door shut.

"Yes," Cam growled, grabbing Dave for another kiss, longer and deeper this time.

"Food arrived a little while ago." Dave was panting now. They both were. "It's in the kitchen."

Can shook his head. "Later."

Jesus help him. Lust had reduced him to single-word conversation. But it wasn't blind lust. He hadn't felt this way toward Alex. Not even Albert had stirred this kind of intensity.

This is what it's supposed to feel like.

Thankfully, Dave didn't protest or make any suggestions about taking it slow. Instead, he took Cam's mouth again, sucking at his lower lip while walking backward in measured, cautious steps, leading Cam toward a sunken den with plush carpet and the longest, widest couch Cam had ever seen.

They fell together in a move so impossibly smooth that Cam might have laughed about it being telepathically choreographed. Except he was too wrapped up in the feel of Dave's body half beneath his, firm chest muscles pressing against Cam's own through the layers of their shirts, the hair on Dave's arm catching on Cam's as he ran his hands down Cam's back.

The sound of Dave grunting as Cam's tongue slipped into his mouth made Cam moan in response, and suddenly Dave's hands were gripping him, shifting Cam until their bodies were aligned from chin to thighs.

Both of them let out long, loud groans at the full-body contact. If not for their clothes, their fully engorged erections would be kissing right now.

It felt incredible, but Cam wanted more. He wanted to feel *everything*.

He pushed himself up enough to move his hand over Dave's chest, sliding down the soft cotton of Dave's T-shirt until he reached the hem, then slipped beneath it.

His fingers on Dave's skin.

Dave hissed out a breath as Cam stroked his palm upward.

Warm and ridged with muscle, touching Dave's stomach was like fondling Heaven.

Rather oddly, that thought only magnified the heady rush of pleasure he was experiencing.

Dave seemed to sense that some of the urgency had dropped off and Cam was now more interested in exploring, because he reached down and grabbed the hem of his T-shirt before pulling it off and tossing it to the floor. Then he lay back, one arm crooked to form a pillow beneath his head while the other hung lazily off the edge of the cushion.

He looked up at Cam as if to say, *Have at me.*

Cam did.

He touched, rubbed, and licked—oh, sweet mercy, Dave tasted good—every inch of skin on Dave's chest, nuzzling into his neck and under his arms, practically leaving friction burns in some places because of their impossible appeal.

Like the section of Dave's lower belly that was paler than the rest of him—the two exposed inches beneath his belly button that were heart-stoppingly firm and yet vulnerably soft at the same time.

Or the stark hollows where Dave's collarbone jutted out on either side of his neck, the low lighting in the room creating enticing shadows that seemed made for Cam's mouth to drink up.

Dave was quiescent, for the most part, making sounds of encouragement and occasionally reaching up to give Cam an anchoring caress. But when Cam moved up Dave's neck, pressing open-mouthed kisses to his jawline before dragging his lips over Dave's, Dave rose up, pushing Cam's shirt off as well.

His hands were everywhere, with just the right pressure, and Cam melted back against the cushions, feet on the floor, as Dave's touches grew more aggressive, his kisses more demanding. This time, Dave knelt on the floor as he worked his mouth down Cam's body, his dark hair shining as he dipped lower, lower . . .

Dave's hand went up Cam's thigh, palm skating over the bulge in his pants, making him groan with desperate need. A moment later, Dave's fingertips were tugging at Cam's waistband, a suggestion more than anything.

Dave paused and looked up at him. "Is this okay?" he whispered.

Cam swallowed hard. "Yeah." He nodded for emphasis, but Dave was already pulling everything off—pants, boxers, even Cam's socks. His achingly hard shaft sprang up as soon as it was freed, and after Dave pushed Cam's pants to the side, he rocked back slightly, eyes roaming over Cam's nude body. After a second, Dave hummed in clear appreciation.

"Beautiful," he murmured.

What happened next made Cam feel like he was swimming through a pool of hazy, viscous liquid. It was impossible for his heart to be working this hard and yet feel like he couldn't move a centimeter.

Dave rubbed over the hairs on Cam's upper thigh, the prickle of the strands as they caught in Dave's fingers and pulled Cam's skin heightening his arousal. His penis jerked slightly in response, and Dave brought the other hand up to wrap around the base of his shaft, as though taming some uncooperative animal. The tight squeeze of Dave's fingers made Cam *feel* animalistic. He even let out a long, low bellow at the contact, like a beast sounding the alarm.

Dave stroked the swollen, hard flesh upward as he brought his mouth forward to slowly lick the tip of Cam's cock.

"Oh sweet Lord," Cam whispered.

Watching Dave do something like this to him was so heady, it was painful. His balls tightened so fast that when Dave trailed his free hand over the top of Cam's thigh and down between his legs to squeeze the taut sac, Cam began to fear he might not last longer than a few more seconds.

He sucked in a sharp, nervous breath and reached out, fingers fluttering a bit before settling into Dave's hair, curling in to feel the softness. But it was a bare second, the blink of an eye, before he gently pushed Dave's head up and away from the roiling pressure between his legs.

"I need—" he gasped "—just a moment."

Dave rocked back until he was sitting on his heels. "Too much?"

Cam swallowed. Nodded. It had probably been obvious well before he'd said something. The skin of his penis was stretched so tight that the veins were popping out in thick, angry ropes over the shaft, the head flushed dark purple. Drops of clear fluid were practically streaming out of the tip, making him feel slick and sticky and much too sensitive.

Dave slowly unwrapped his fingers from the base of Cam's shaft and withdrew his hand.

Cam sucked in a shallow breath, though it was as deep as he could manage right then. "Maybe I can try . . . maybe we'll start with you." His voice cracked as he spoke. "I have to calm down."

Dave let out a surprised-sounding laugh. "I don't think I've ever heard that before." He looked at Cam for a long moment, seeming to study him, then nodded. "Okay." He levered himself up and flopped back onto the couch, body touching Cam's on the side.

That feels so good.

Cam considered covering himself up again by sliding on his boxers, but quickly decided against it. It would be a futile task, anyway, given how erect he was. Instead, he twisted until he was leaning over Dave, then kissed him. A grounding before he went on to the next unknown.

He pulled away, feeling more stable, but he lacked the finesse to work past his nerves enough to trail kisses down Dave's chest. Instead, he wriggled away inelegantly, then practically fell to his knees between Dave's open legs, his hands slapping down hard on Dave's thighs with the impact.

How embarrassing.

But when he looked up at Dave, mouth open to apologize, there was no judgment in the other man's face. Only slack-jawed desire. Appreciation for Cam despite—or perhaps including—his inexperience.

It emboldened Cam enough to tug Dave's sweatpants and boxers off in one rough motion, shoving them all to the floor before sitting back and looking his fill.

Holy God.

There was a fully naked man lying in front of him. In the flesh. Not an online image, not a lurid fantasy. This man had kissed him and given him pleasure. This man had listened and understood.

A part of Cam feared he would awaken any minute to find that none of this had ever happened.

He brought his hand forward and ran it lightly over Dave's belly, ending in the nest of tight, curly hairs. Cam gently combed his fingers through the curls, the circle of his thumb and index finger narrowing until they formed a tight ring at the base of Dave's beautiful cock.

It was as elegant as the rest of him. Long. Not too thick. Beautifully veined, as though he'd been sculpted by an artist. The skin was lighter there than the rest of his body, taking on a ruddy hue with blood engorging his shaft, the deep pink of the head practically beckoning Cam.

He leaned forward, his mouth scant inches from the tip, and again looked up at Dave, who groaned.

Cam smiled shyly. "I, uh— Tell me if I do something wrong. Or if I don't do something right." Maybe he sounded like a moron giving both of those conditions, but they weren't the same things.

He licked his lips, and Dave groaned again, louder this time. "Cam. You're already doing it so right."

Cam nodded, then dipped his head. *Enough stalling.*

His mouth slid around the head, his eyes rolling back in his head as the sweet, spongy tip touched his tongue. He could hear Dave breathing hard. Cam worked his mouth lower, sucking as he went, pressing his tongue against the underside of Dave's shaft, just the way Cam liked it too.

"Cam." It was Dave's turn to bring his free hand up to rest atop Cam's head, fingers curling into Cam's scalp as his hips jerked upward.

Cam pulled back abruptly, trying not to gag from the blunt stab on the back of his throat.

Dave was already curling his body forward, caressing Cam's face to soothe him. "Sorry. Oh, man, I'm sorry. It was just so good, I—"

But Cam pushed Dave to lie back again, shaking his head. "It's okay. I need to learn."

"You're a natural," Dave panted, lips turned up in a semblance of a smile.

Cam took a deep breath and this time when he took Dave into his mouth, he went nearly all the way down in one steady motion.

The praise he was getting from Dave was coming fast and wild.

"So good. That feels so good. You know exactly how to touch me. That's it. That's right. I love it. God, Cam, I love it."

It spurred Cam on. He set a rhythm of up and down, sucking and squeezing, bringing his tongue to swirl around the head, dipping into the slit at the top of Dave's beautiful, straining erection. After a few minutes, Dave's head lolled back, grunts coming from deep in his chest with every stroke.

Cam felt Dave's thighs tighten a second before Dave groaned, "I'm gonna come."

He pumped his hips upward, but Cam was ready for it, helping Dave along with a hand at the bottom of his shaft and mouth sealed over the top.

Dave came with a brief shout, his cock pulsing over and over in Cam's mouth.

Cam swallowed everything he could, his eyes closing with pleasure and pride as Dave finished and relaxed, sinking back into the couch as though every part of him had suddenly grown too heavy to exist without support.

He'd done that. He'd just made a man boneless with pleasure.

One last lick and he pulled his mouth away with a soft *pop*, then wiped the back of his hand over his lips as discreetly as he could manage. Was that okay? He hoped he hadn't just breached some unspoken etiquette by doing that.

But Dave didn't give him any more time for insecurities to creep in.

He lifted a hand languorously and gestured Cam forward. "Come here and kiss me."

The way it felt to drape his nude body over Dave's equally naked one nearly had Cam coming right then. They rolled around for a few minutes, Dave licking at Cam's mouth almost in reminder that Cam had just swallowed a part of him.

Cam was so turned on that, by the time Dave maneuvered him to lie flat on the couch, a throw pillow beneath his head, he knew his impending orgasm would be epic. Like nothing he'd ever experienced before.

Dave insinuated one knee between Cam's legs and braced himself on the floor with the other foot. A second later, Dave's lips closed over the engorged head of Cam's cock, the feeling of intense pressure making Cam groan in agonized relief.

"This is going to be fast. So fast." Cam was straining, gritting his teeth and unable to tear his gaze from the rapturous sight of Dave's mouth on his shaft, working its way downward with the perfect degree of hot, wet suction.

Dave slid back up and completely off. Cam whimpered.

"Good." Dave laughed and winked at Cam before taking him again, going deep, sucking hard, playing with his pulled-up sac.

It was impossible to hold back. Barely thirty seconds later, Cam was practically screaming with his climax. It was the most intense orgasm he'd ever had, as though his entire soul were being poured out of that tiny slit in the head of his dick. His body jerked, shuddering, nearly coming apart with the fearful power of his release.

Dave crawled up onto the couch after Cam finally stopped shuddering and pulled over them a light throw that had been folded in a basket near the coffee table. They were lying facing one another on the seat cushions, feet tangled together as they lazed. Dave smelled faintly of soap and sweat, and Cam dipped his head to the curve of Dave's neck, inhaling deeply.

There was something so intimate about knowing the scent of another person. Cam could feel it feeding a latent arousal that had everything to do with this particular man.

Dave stretched and made a contented sound. "Well, hell, Cam. That was . . . wow. Amazing."

His words came out on a drawl, and Cam laughed. "You almost sound like me."

Dave chuckled, and a second later Cam caught up to what Dave had actually said.

"Was it really good?"

He immediately wanted to smack himself in the face for letting his insecurity come out like that. And, at the same time, he argued with himself that he was old enough to both be honest and to demand honest answers to things he genuinely wanted to know.

Dave pulled Cam close and rumbled, "Really. That was intense. I don't think I've ever experienced something quite that arousing."

Cam was taken aback by Dave's statement, wanting to believe it but strongly doubting it. "But you have so much more experience." He snorted. "You have *experience*, period."

Dave laughed. "Experience isn't always meaningful."

Cam didn't push him to explain. He wasn't even sure he wanted to know the details. He was curious, but *experience*, no matter what Dave said, was still intimidating.

Luckily, Dave continued. "You probably saw it at Ce-lo, right? How those guys are only after one thing. It's meaningless. When you're in that club, though, it *feels* like it's important because everyone is treating anonymous sex as something valuable—it's the end goal of every man in there."

Cam coughed, and Dave laughed and added, "Okay, maybe not *every* man." He grinned at Cam, who couldn't resist giving him a hard, quick kiss of joy.

Dave shifted, bending his elbow to prop his head up on his hand, and his face grew somewhat serious. "Places like Ce-lo and the guys who go there, that's only a fraction of real life. I mean, for me personally, I was a huge nerd in high school. The only reason I came out so early is because I barely socialized anyway, and the few friends I had cared more about working on their computers than my sexuality. It was a nonissue almost from the start."

"I'd like to believe it," Cam whispered. "But I'm not sure what's normal and what's not. The conversations I had with friends back when we were teenagers and what I see on TV are the only reference points I have about modern sex. And when it comes to relationships—"

Neither man needed to hear any more. Cam knew it, but couldn't seem to stop himself until Dave rolled forward a bit and nipped at Cam's shoulder, a bite bordering on painful.

It was almost humorous, this unorthodox approach to shutting up another person.

"Cam, I'm fifty-one years old. I don't need to hop from one bed to another." He rested his chin on Cam's arm and gave a small shrug. "That's never been my style, anyway, even when I was *twenty*-one. For what it's worth, for all that you might feel out of your element when it comes to us, this level of—of *feeling* is new to me too. Not even with—"

Dave stopped abruptly, but Cam couldn't keep his curiosity at bay. "Even with what?" he prodded.

Dave didn't respond, and after a long moment, Cam grew embarrassed. He was about to tell Dave to forget it when Dave suddenly spoke again.

"Until two years ago, I was with someone. We were together for fifteen years. I loved him, and I thought we were going to be together forever. But I still never felt for him this kind of . . ." He rocked his head slightly from side to side as if searching for the right word.

Fifteen years. Dave had been in a long-term relationship. Practically married.

It made sense. Dave was that kind of guy. What Cam didn't understand was— "Why did you two split up?"

He watched as Dave's throat worked in a hard swallow.

"He turned fifty, freaked out, and went in a rather desperate search to reclaim his youth."

That didn't sound good.

"He cheated on me with four different men in the span of a week," Dave continued. "And those are just the ones I actually know about."

Cam whistled.

Dave gave a grunt of wry laughter. "Exactly. It was . . . not a great time in my life. I'd just retired with visions of spending *more* time with Srikanth, not having him go off the rails like that and end fifteen years together in such an explosive way." He sighed. "But I had Pedro and Richard and long hours on my bicycle. I got through it."

Jesus above. That certainly explained why Pedro and Richard had seemed so protective of Dave at certain points.

"I'm sorry." Cam reached out his hand in search of Dave's. Their fingers brushed. Entwined. Cam squeezed gently.

Dave stared at him for a second, his expression serious, then closed the distance between them for a soft, lingering kiss so full of sweetness that Cam felt it all the way to his toes.

Dave pulled back and gave him a lopsided smile. "Hey. Are you hungry?"

The sudden shift in topic threw Cam off for a beat, but he recovered quickly and was glad for the distraction. He got the feeling neither he nor Dave was ready to get even more serious with their conversation . . . or whatever was going on between them.

"Last time you asked me that, we ended up not eating anything," he teased.

Dave laughed. "True. But I'm not sorry."

They got dressed, stealing kisses between pulling and tugging clothes on and up their bodies, then padded into Dave's expansive kitchen. Dave rewarmed the food while Cam opened a bottle of wine, and they ate dinner at the long bar that separated the food prep space from a bigger dining area. Cam made a conscious effort to talk about anything *except* what they'd just done in the living room, which wasn't really that difficult, in the end. He enjoyed talking to Dave, and this time they covered space travel (Dave wanted to take a space tourism flight, Cam thought it was a death wish) and gardening (Cam named most of the plants in Dave's front yard, while Dave could barely tell the difference between a tree and a bush).

They watched a movie afterward on the very couch where they'd both succumbed earlier to rapturous pleasure, but they were quiet and still for the entire movie, leaning into one another as they watched two young people fall madly in love.

Cam didn't stay the night.

Dave had invited him to, but Cam thought it would be best if they didn't get to that point just yet. It felt too intimate, even if all they did was sleep.

Their kiss good night, though, was long and leisurely, as if to make up somehow for the lack of the rest of the night together.

And when Cam woke up the next morning in his own bed, he found himself in a euphoric state of having *gotten it right*, and thought that, perhaps in this case, experience meant *everything*.

1993

"Cam! Cam, come quick!"

Cam raced into the front room at the sound of LaVerne's urgent calls.

"What is it? Is everything—" He stopped short at the sight of LaVerne sitting on the floor, holding Elijah upright on his short eleven-month-old legs. There didn't seem to be anything wrong.

"He just took two steps!" LaVerne squealed.

Elijah smiled up at Cam from where he stood—unsteadily, it seemed, holding on to LaVerne's proffered fingers.

Cam smiled back.

If there was one thing in his life that he would never view as a mistake, or the wrong fit, it was his son.

"Think he'll do it again?" He squatted down and held out his arms toward Elijah, who was still grinning at him, showing off two small front teeth in an otherwise toothless, drooling mouth.

Cam thought it was the most beautiful sight he'd ever seen.

He watched, riveted, as Elijah opened one fist, then the other, releasing his grip on LaVerne before reaching his chubby hands toward Cam.

One step.

Two steps.

Three and—

Elijah dropped on his diapered bottom, then crawled the rest of the way to Cam, where he was met with hugs and excited praise.

Cam was laughing over his son's accomplishment when he looked over at LaVerne, who was staring at the two of them with a funny look on her face.

"I can't believe he's walking," she whispered. "He's growing more independent every day. Soon he'll be walking away from us and into his own life."

Whoa. That had certainly taken a turn for the dramatic. Cam trod lightly around the shift in her emotions as he held Elijah close. "First steps are a big deal. But we shouldn't get ahead of him. It's not fair to him or to us. We can all afford to take a little time to savor this new world." He laughed quietly. "Pretty soon he'll be off and running after every last thing he wants, and we'll spend our days chasing him and wishing he weren't so accomplished."

"Never!" She leaned over to swat at him, missing him by a mile, then choked out a laugh. "You're right, Cam. Of course you're right. I just felt so much pride at seeing him that I ended up overwhelmed and . . . well, a little afraid, if I'm being completely honest."

Completely honest. What would that feel like? And what would it take for him to reach that point?

He certainly knew what it was like to be overwhelmed. Afraid. But honesty wasn't in the cards for men like him.

It was probably for the best.

He scooped up Elijah in one arm and offered his free hand to LaVerne to help her up.

"Come on. Let's go show off this guy to the grandparents."

After all, first steps were a big deal.

Chapter Ten

E lijah called later that morning, and Cam found himself unable to keep his happiness from bubbling over into their greetings.

"Sounds like the big city has been treating you well," Elijah said.

"Yeah." Cam leaned back in his chair and thought of Dave. "Really well."

"Good to hear . . ."

Cam waited. A second later, Elijah asked, "Dad, I—I hope you don't take this the wrong way. But what do you *do* all day?"

Though Cam couldn't see his son's face, the confusion in Elijah's voice was coming through loud and clear, and he couldn't resist laughing. Had he ever been that young? Somehow, he didn't think so.

"Have you been wondering this for the past month?"

There was a brief, telling pause before Elijah admitted, "Yeah. I didn't want to ask you before, but you seem really happy today, so . . . yeah, anyway. I guess I'm pretty curious."

For a moment, Cam wavered. The step he'd taken with Dave last night felt so significant that it almost burst out of him—happiness that was too big to hold back. But he managed to keep himself in check. It wouldn't do to destroy his chance at these couple of months of bliss.

"I read," he told Elijah. "I signed up for that embroidery class, believe it or not. I go once a week on Tuesdays. I walk every day for at least an hour and sometimes I just sit in silence on the back balcony."

It was all true, anyway. Just because it omitted Dave didn't mean it wasn't true.

It felt dishonest, though, and more and more Cam was struggling against the weight of his lifelong lies. Happiness had a way of making lies seem . . . immature.

"That sounds, uh, relaxing," Elijah managed, but Cam could hear disbelief.

He chuckled. "I know it's not my usual style. But this is a few months away from reality, and I'm taking advantage of it. I've spent my life working hard. I'm taking a break for a little while before I go back to who I used to be."

Who he used to be. His joy deflated somewhat, because the reminder sounded so—so—*depressing.*

But, then again, who was he now, barely a month away from his old life? And who was he still? It wasn't as though he were planning to stay in this place for long. It shouldn't have mattered.

He brought a hand up to pinch the bridge of his nose. He didn't want these things in his mind right now. He'd been so *happy* a moment ago.

"Yeah, well, about that. The going back part . . ." Elijah stopped again, putting Cam on edge. It seemed that both of them were acting unexpectedly today.

"What is it?"

Elijah must have heard the demand in Cam's voice, because there was no more hesitation. "A guy came in about an hour ago and gave me his card. He represents a company that's looking to buy up the whole place. Existing stock, machinery, everything."

"Someone wants to buy my—our business?" He was shocked. He didn't think anyone outside of the county knew about McGhee Feed & Grain.

Elijah huffed. "The business is yours, Dad. You don't need to pretend otherwise for my sake."

We're both self-made men.

"But yeah. Someone wants to buy it. I looked up the company this guy represents. It's a huge agricultural operation. They do hybrid strains and hyper-resistant crops, from what I can find online."

Cam frowned. "You mean genetically modified stuff?"

"I think so. The language on their website dances around it, but it sure seems like it."

Cam didn't have real strong feelings about GMO seeds, but he knew enough to proceed with caution. "What did you tell him?"

"I said that you weren't here right now, but I'd have you call him if you're interested."

"Thanks, son."

"*Are* you interested?"

Cam thought about it for a second. He'd never considered it because he'd expected to pass on the business to the next generation. To Elijah, specifically. But he'd never actually asked Elijah whether he wanted to inherit the place.

As much as he criticized the way Bitter pulled them all back, it seemed he was guilty of making the same assumption about Elijah's future that he'd made about his own.

An assumption he was beginning to question all too frequently.

But, right now, it wasn't about him.

"Do you want to take it over when I retire?" No better approach than simply asking.

"No." Elijah didn't hesitate, and it both pained and relieved Cam to know that his son hadn't even had to take time to think it over. "I wouldn't have known if I hadn't come back to work here as an adult, though," Elijah explained. "When I helped you back in high school, I thought it was kind of fun, acting like a grown-up around the store. But after years living somewhere else, the idea of coming back to Bitter for the rest of my life . . ."

Now Elijah hesitated, probably worried that he'd hurt Cam's feelings.

"I understand." And Cam did. Fifty-four years in that town and after only a month away, he got it.

"I'll think about it, then," he told Elijah, but after he hung up, he took the piece of paper with the contact information for the buyer and shoved it in an empty cookie jar in the kitchen, then sealed the lid over it.

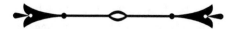

Saturday morning found Cam sitting in the coffee shop, waiting nervously for Dave to show up. He wanted to get his fill before a week went by without seeing one another.

Dave walked in and made a beeline for Cam, who stood up to see him.

"You're a sight for sore eyes." Dave's eyes were roaming all over Cam's face and body, making him feel warm. "I didn't expect to see you today."

"Georgia won't arrive until the afternoon, and I—" He was going to say that he had some time, but that wasn't really the reason he was there. *Be honest.* "I wanted to see you again before she got here."

Dave gave him a broad smile and stroked a hand down Cam's arm. "I'm going to go get something to drink. Sit with us today?"

"Yes." It came out quiet and breathy, so obviously full of desire that neither of them moved for a long moment.

The sound of someone clearing his throat had them jumping apart. Cam hadn't realized they'd moved so close together, but was grateful to Pedro for the interruption. They might have ended up making a scene in the café.

Pedro and Richard set their cups down, and before Dave could head over to the counter to place an order, Pedro shoved a mug in his direction. "We got you covered," he told Dave. "Can I get you something too?" he asked Cam.

Cam raised his own mug. "I'm good. But thank you."

Pedro nodded and all four men sat. Richard seemed even more withdrawn than usual, and Cam raised a brow at Dave while subtly tipping his head toward Richard.

"How's that knee now?" Dave asked Richard, effectively answering Cam's unspoken question.

"Same," Richard grunted. "Goddamn it."

"A couple weeks of rest will help," Pedro offered, and Cam could tell he'd already said it more than once.

"I used to be able to ride through muscle pain," Richard groused. "It's like a switch got flipped when I turned forty-five last month."

Cam bit back a laugh. Since his midforties, he'd experienced the same thing. Injuries, illness, everything took longer to recover from. But he'd had a few more years to get used to it than Richard, who seemed as much in shock about the general decline of his body as he was frustrated with his current pain.

"Welcome to middle age." Cam lifted his cup of coffee in salute. "Where both opportunity and pitfalls abound."

The table laughed. Pedro brought his cup to Cam's and clinked them together. "Too true." He set his cup down and leaned back in his chair. "As the oldest one here, I think it's only fair to warn all of you that the degeneration only speeds up." He grinned. "But the peace of mind is worth the pain."

Peace of mind.

That brought Cam up short. He didn't have to think about it to know he didn't have that.

He was middle-aged. Well into it. Was he supposed to have peace of mind?

Under the table, he felt Dave's hand land on his knee and gently squeeze before redirecting the conversation to an article Richard was writing about discrimination in Texas schools.

They talked for a while about some of the information Richard had uncovered so far and where he would take the story before Richard turned to Cam. "How's your grain operation doing with you away?"

Cam took solace in Dave's hand, which was still curled around his knee. "My son called on Thursday. Seems someone came in and offered to buy the business. He's from a big GMO corporation."

The three other men made sounds of surprise, and at first Cam assumed it was because of the news that Cam was a father. But it became clear quite quickly that revelation was secondary to the purchase offer.

Pedro drummed his fingers on the tabletop as he stared at Cam. "Have you considered selling in the past?"

He shook his head. "I thought I'd have it forever, then pass it on to my son." He snorted. "Except he's already been running the place for a month and apparently that's enough experience to make him think I should sell it."

Dave turned to him. "Really?"

Cam nodded. "I was a little surprised, but not as much as I probably should have been." He looked down at the liquid in his cup. "It's amazing what a little time away will do to perspective."

"So you think you'll sell?" Richard asked.

"It sounds like something worth considering," Pedro added.

Cam shrugged. "Real estate isn't exactly booming in Bitter. I don't know if I could get a reasonable price for the house. If I couldn't sell it, I wouldn't want to let go of the only thing that keeps me going in that town."

"But do you *want* to go back to it?" Pedro's question felt a lot more personal than Cam had expected, and he was pretty sure it had everything to do with protecting Dave.

Cam couldn't fault Pedro's instincts, at least. He *was* planning to return home.

But did he want to?

He was quiet for a long moment, and all the men sipped their coffee out of polite consideration.

Finally, he shrugged. "I don't know." And then, because he was feeling the weight of his middle age bearing down, counteracting the reassuring heaviness of Dave's hand on his body, he added, "I've found in my life that often what I want doesn't really matter. Sometimes, the choices I make are first and foremost about simply staying alive. In my experience, actually *living* . . . well, that's a luxury."

There was a collective moment of silence at his words, as though by some unspoken agreement they were all paying homage to the life they could have had—that each of them in turn had already passed over—before Dave piped up and once again shifted the topic to something less intense.

It occurred to Cam that all too soon, Dave wouldn't be in his life anymore to smooth things over when they got too rough.

He wondered what that meant for his future.

1995

Sickle cell anemia.

Cam stared at the doctor, who was sitting on the wheeled stool in the exam room, looking solemn after having just delivered the diagnosis.

LaVerne was cradling her abdomen as though trying to prevent the baby inside from hearing the words.

"I was looking back at Mrs. McGhee's medical records, and it seems that she's exhibited symptoms for years—decades, in fact."

The doctor frowned, his pale skin furrowing into already-deep lines although he was young. A few years younger than Cam and LaVerne, probably. So different from Dr. Winslow, the elderly Englishman who had served as LaVerne's family doctor as well as the attending physician when Elijah was born.

Everyone in town had gone to Dr. Winslow, even though his offices were an hour's drive away. For decades he'd been the only doctor in the area willing to treat black people, and he was revered by the entire community.

No one questioned Dr. Winslow.

But he'd retired last year and had been replaced with this baby-faced boy, freshly certified and clearly appalled by the lack of knowledge applied to LaVerne's condition.

Under other circumstances, Cam would have sneered at him and left to look for another physician, but LaVerne was seven months pregnant with their second child and had spent the past two days barely able to move. This morning, Cam had insisted on bringing LaVerne in to find out if something was wrong.

Well, they'd certainly found out.

Dr. Phillips continued, "But I don't see any indication or record of a test for sickle cell anemia. Is that correct?"

He was looking at LaVerne earnestly, almost apologetically.

She nodded. "Dr. Winslow told me I had a weak constitution and would need to rest more than other people from time to time. There never seemed to be a need for a test."

Dr. Phillips's mouth tightened in obvious anger, but he didn't say anything to disparage the retired doctor. He must know, even after a short time working in this community, what Dr. Winslow had meant to the people here.

Even if he'd been so disastrously wrong.

"What does this mean?" Cam ventured to ask. "What can we— Will it harm the baby?"

LaVerne gasped softly and kept her eyes riveted on Dr. Phillips while blindly groping to the side for Cam's hand.

He took it, holding his breath while waiting for the doctor to reply.

"Right now, the percentage of sickle cells in her blood is still low enough that I think the baby will be okay." He looked down at the chart he held and studied it. "To be honest, the low percentage might be why you've weathered the disease so well. But I'd like to see you in for regular monitoring, Mrs. McGhee."

"What do you mean?" LaVerne's fingers were digging into Cam's palm. "This is 'weathering it well'?"

Dr. Phillips jerked his head up from the papers on his lap. He looked slightly alarmed, as though belatedly registering that his delivery had left something to be desired.

"I, well—" He gaped for a moment, then continued. "Usually, without proper early intervention, sufferers of sickle cell anemia can expect to live into their teens." He sounded like he was reciting from a textbook. "But you've obviously surpassed that, and your bloodwork points to fairly healthy, functioning organs. If things continue this way, there's no reason you shouldn't expect to live into middle age."

"Middle . . . age?" LaVerne squeaked.

Cam wanted to smack Dr. Phillips for implying that LaVerne could expect to live only until her children were still too young to lose her.

"Dr. Phillips, would you please give us a moment?" Cam kept his voice as neutral as he could, and the doctor seemed relieved to be dismissed.

Once he'd left the room, Cam twisted to face LaVerne, still holding her hand. She was staring down at the floor.

"Hey." He dipped his head, trying to get her to look at him.

Slowly, she raised her eyes to his. Tears were dripping silently down her cheeks.

"I suppose it's too much to believe that I'll beat the odds again and live to see my children walk down the aisle? Hold my grandchildren. Sit in a wheelchair with white hair and look at old photos and—" Her words were choked off by a sob.

From what Dr. Phillips had said, it *was* too much to hope for. The test results were conclusive. It wasn't as though they could pretend she didn't have the disease. And all the signs were there. Had been for decades. They *both* knew the dreams she'd just shared most likely wouldn't come true.

But what dreams might yet?

There was no knowing that. And there was nothing he could say. Instead, Cam leaned forward and put his arms around her, letting her curl over her belly and cry for all the experiences yet to come, as well as for those that never would.

Chapter Eleven

"Dad!" Georgia jumped out of her beat-up sedan and raced forward, practically slamming into Cam as she wrapped her arms tightly around him. "Oh, Daddy, I've missed you."

It was half past two that Saturday afternoon, and Cam had been home for only an hour when Georgia had rung him from the parking lot of the apartment complex. He'd run out of the apartment just in time to see her opening the door of the car to climb out.

He hugged her back and kissed her forehead, closing his eyes for a second and remembering when she used to be so tiny that he could pick her up and swing her in the air.

"Georgia. I'm glad you made it safely." He let go and only then took a moment to study her. "You look more grown-up since I saw you last."

She rolled her eyes, but was smiling. "You saw me over Christmas."

"That must be why. You're three months older. Makes sense," he teased.

"You're such a dork," she laughed. She gestured around the complex parking lot. "By the way, can I just say how much your place looks like my college campus?"

He let out a bark of laughter. "With the amount of money that school is charging, I kind of hope your campus is nicer than my apartment."

"Da-ad." She rolled her eyes. "I do have a partial scholarship, you know."

He reached out and nipped her chin with his fingers. "I know. And I'm proud of you for that."

"I know it's still expensive, though," she quickly added. "And I really, really appreciate you sending me to college. Elijah was on my case yesterday about not having gone to one of the military academies and saved you some money. Why can't he get off my back, already? I'm graduating in two months!"

Elijah had been pestering her? And about money, of all things. After their conversation about the potential buyer for the business, did he think that Cam was hurting for funds? Cam made a mental note to follow up with his son about it after Georgia had gone.

"Come on, forget about it. You're on vacation now." Cam opened the rear door of the car and grabbed her bag from the backseat. "Let's go inside." He guided her forward, then followed her up the stairs and opened the door to his apartment. "It's this one."

She stepped inside and took it all in. "Dad." She giggled then looked over her shoulder at him. "You live in a *bachelor pad*."

He snorted. "I don't think it's too different from our house in Bitter."

She did a circle, her eyes roaming over the room as she turned. "No, I guess the furniture is similar. Maybe in that sense it's like home. But all the little touches—pictures on the wall, knickknacks on the shelves, soft things like pillows and throws and stuff. They're not here." Her tone was wistful.

He cast a glance around too. Maybe it *was* kind of sterile. But it was also *temporary*. He hadn't considered decorating a place he planned to be in for only a handful of months.

"I like it, though!" she chirped, her eyes going wide and overly sincere. She was trying too hard to make him feel better. "I'm sorry. I didn't mean to insult your place. It's a good size." She nodded as though it would make her words sound more positive. "Lots of light."

Cam huffed out a laugh. "Oh, Georgia. C'mere."

He held out his arms, and she stepped into them, speaking into the fabric of his T-shirt. "I really am sorry."

He released her from the hug, but chucked her under the chin—for old time's sake—before letting her go completely. "I forgive you. It's probably a lot for you to take in, and that's okay. It's never gonna be like the house in Bitter. Not leastways because your mom was responsible for all that—" he wiggled his fingers in the air, trying to indicate the décor "—little-touch stuff. I'd imagine our house would look a lot more like this apartment if she hadn't been around."

Georgia nodded emphatically. "Exactly. It's a bachelor pad."

He laughed. Apparently her remorse didn't keep her from speaking her mind.

He was proud of her for that. And he supposed she had a point. He *was* a bachelor.

But then, Dave was one too, even if they were dating, and Dave's house was warmly welcoming. Homey.

He missed Dave.

This was not good. He wasn't supposed to miss a man he'd been seeing for such a short time and with whom there could never be a real future.

"Where should I put my stuff?"

Georgia's question spurred Cam back into action, and he chided himself for mooning over Dave. Too much of this and she'd start getting uncomfortably suspicious. He led her into the small second bedroom, furnished with only a futon and a flimsy chipboard nightstand.

Georgia chortled. "Bachelor. Pad."

Her glee at teasing him was too *silly* to be angry over, but Cam had to remind himself that she wasn't trying to insult his integrity or infer that he was trying to recapture lost youth. He knew what it was like to be young—Georgia was there now, and she could do anything, *be* anything simply by virtue of having her whole life ahead of her.

His had already been decided. He'd lived whatever greatness he'd been intended to have, which wasn't exactly noteworthy. But then, if he'd followed his heart of hearts back when youth was on his side, he never would have had Elijah and Georgia.

And he certainly couldn't imagine life without them.

Georgia tossed her purse onto the futon and turned to him, still grinning. "So, what do you want to do this week?"

Ah, youth.

"We could see the city. There's a nice park with a great view of the skyline." *That Dave showed me.* "And I think you'd enjoy touring the capitol, doing some hiking, things like that."

She nodded. "Sounds cool."

"We could drive up to Round Rock one morning and get donuts," he added.

"Yeah!" Her reply was more enthusiastic this time. Georgia had always had a sweet tooth.

"Okay," he laughed. "That's about all I can come up with right now, but there are a couple of girls in my embroidery class on Tuesday—you're welcome to join that—and they might have a few suggestions for things to do. Maybe you can even go out with them."

"Embroidery!" Georgia guffawed, but immediately stopped when she looked at his face. "Are you being *serious*?"

"Why wouldn't I be?"

She looked uncomfortable for a second, but then reverted back to her impish self. "Whoa. Who are you and what have you done with my father?"

Her accusation, even if made in jest, had him all fidgety. If she only knew the secrets he'd been keeping his entire life.

Luckily, Georgia didn't seem to notice his agitation, because in the next second she clapped her hands together gleefully. "Let's go get you a phone!"

Oh, right. He'd told her they would do that as soon as she arrived.

Twenty minutes later, they were standing in a wireless provider's shop, browsing devices. Well, Georgia was browsing—*oohing* and *ahhing* over this functionality and that design. Cam was following her, hands in pockets, wishing he'd never agreed to this but trying to put a happy face on it nonetheless. For Georgia's sake.

Although . . . being able to call Dave whenever he wanted would be nice. Being able to take pictures of Dave and carry them around to look at whenever he wanted . . . so nice.

"How about this one?" He walked back to one of the devices that Georgia had practically fainted over with excitement.

Her eyes lit up, but then she frowned. "You said you didn't want anything fancy."

"I changed my mind."

"You *changed your mind*?" Georgia was gaping at him.

He kept his tone as light as he could manage when he replied, "Yeah. I guess I have changed."

She stared at him slightly longer than what could be considered normal, eyes narrowed as if trying to solve the puzzle he'd put in front of her. He held his breath, wondering if she would ask. Wondering if he secretly wanted her to.

But she must have decided he was playing around, because eventually she rolled her eyes in mock annoyance and grabbed a salesman.

After they checked out, Georgia handed him the box with a flourish. "Your new life awaits."

He stared down at the package he was holding.

If only it were that easy—a nice, neat container that he could take out and put away again at will.

Isn't that what you're doing, though?

Come July, he'd be packing up his time with Dave and heading back to Bitter with a box of memories to stow away.

He didn't like it. Of course he didn't. But what other choice did he have?

"Dave Montoya."

Sitting on his bed, Cam closed his eyes for a moment at the sound of Dave's delicious voice through the phone. He sounded so sexy that Cam wished he could say something seductive in greeting, but he knew it wouldn't come out right.

So he settled for a low, "Dave, it's Cam."

"Cam?" The happy surprise evident from Dave put Cam at ease. "Where are you calling from?"

"My new cell phone."

Cam heard a soft laugh on the other end. "Welcome to the twenty-first century."

"Georgia had to show me how to use it." Cam chuckled. "We had a few hours of tutoring this afternoon. Having a phone like this is actually pretty neat. I drew the line when she wanted to install some game about candy, though."

Dave's laugh was rich and sweet. "Sounds like the visit is going well so far."

"It is. She's grown up a lot." Cam worried his fingers at the hem of his shirt. "But in a lot of ways she's still a child. She's asleep on the couch in the living room—just curled up in a ball and dozed off like she used to do when she was a little girl."

"Sounds like that saying, how the more things change, the more they stay the same."

"Yeah. Something like that." Except that it felt like everything had changed, and Cam wasn't sure how to handle it.

"So what will you guys do tomorrow?"

"I'm taking her to Zilker Park."

"I have fond memories of that park."

Cam blushed. Even after everything they'd done together, it felt so good to have Dave *flirting* with him.

"I do too. But mine are more about the company I was with than the park itself."

Lord save him, he was flirting back, and that felt good too.

They talked for a couple of more minutes before Cam heard movement beyond his closed bedroom door.

"I better say good night. I think Georgia woke up, and I've got to go see if she's okay. I'm glad I got to hear your voice."

"You wanted to hear my voice?"

Cam could hear Dave's smile through the line.

"Yeah. I did."

"That's an excellent way to say good night," Dave purred. "I'll be going to bed thinking about you wanting to hear me."

It was such a simple statement, but the way he said it made the message sound sexual. Cam had to take a deep breath to brace himself long enough to say a simple good-bye.

He hung up with Dave just as Georgia knocked on the door.

"Come in!" he called.

Georgia opened the door, looking groggy and disheveled. "Hey, Daddy. Who were you talking to?"

It didn't matter that she was taller than LaVerne had been or that she was old enough to drive, vote, drink, and live completely independently from him. Cam felt the squeeze of unconditional love wrap around his chest, knocking the air from his lungs at the sight of her like this, so reminiscent of the tousled, bleary-eyed child who used to show up in the door to the master bedroom, asking for comfort after a nightmare.

How could he ever tell her that the father she'd known all her life had been nothing more than a carefully constructed image? How could he rip that comfort away from her?

"Just working on setting up my voice mail," he lied.

She gave him a lopsided smile. "I can help you with it tomorrow. I'm heading to bed now."

"You doing all right? Need anything?"

"No, I'm good. Just tired. I'll use the bathroom real quick first. Sorry I fell asleep on you."

He shook his head. "I don't mind." He got up, crossed the room, and gave her a hug. "Sweet dreams, Georgia."

She might not come to him anymore when she had a nightmare, but he would at least do his best to protect her, protect Elijah, in whatever capacity he could.

Even if the one who could hurt them the most was him.

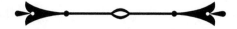

1996

Georgia Ann McGhee was born three weeks early, but Dr. Phillips insisted that had been Georgia's decision and not a function of LaVerne's illness.

Regardless, the birth had taken a lot out of LaVerne, and she was struggling to recover, with initial tests showing that her liver was operating at a less-than-desired level. As a result, Dr. Phillips had insisted that she remain in the hospital awhile longer on IV antibiotics. She wasn't allowed to nurse Georgia, who had come out healthy and hungry.

Cam had never been so worn out in his life. A big operation out of Abilene had bought up thousands of acres near Bitter, and they had turned to McGhee Feed & Grain for their feed. His business was growing by leaps and bounds, which meant he had to pull long hours at the store, trying to manage grain processing, keeping the feed stocked, and making sure the boom didn't lose momentum. But Elijah still needed watching over and someone had to care for Georgia since LaVerne was so weakened.

Thank God his mother and mother-in-law had stepped up and taken over. There was no way he could have kept everything going if they hadn't been around to help.

With the birth of his kids, it should have become easier to hide his sexuality. At least, that's what Cam had thought. But it turned out to be the opposite. Every day Elijah grew and his personality revealed itself, Cam found himself wishing he could be as honest as his son was about his true self. When Georgia had come screaming into the world, Cam had held her and nearly cried over the cruelty of his social prison, and even the exhausting pace of work and home life hadn't assuaged the frantic desire to tell someone—*anyone*—the truth. It was a burden that grew heavier every day, and he *hated* it.

But every time he stopped himself with thoughts about Roger Henderson. Roger was somewhere out there, totally alone. If Roger ever needed help, who would he turn to? If he was even still alive.

Cam hadn't heard anything to the contrary, but then again, he hadn't heard anything, period.

He lifted another sack of feed onto the pallet in the back warehouse and grunted with the strain. It hurt. All of it hurt. It made him feel desperate and angry and, in its own torturous way, so very alone.

But without his family's help, everything would fall apart, anyway.

What choice did he have?

Some secrets were better kept hidden.

Chapter Twelve

C am took Georgia to his embroidery class on Tuesday. He'd taken a few photos to surreptitiously text to Dave (Georgia had taught him how to send messages with images attached), and Dave texted back, *I never realized how being a good dad is incredibly sexy. Can't wait to see you again.*

Cam had to take a moment before his eyes could focus past the haze of lust.

His hair was graying, his muscles weren't as big or defined as they once were, and on rainy days, his knee cracked when he walked. But he'd never felt more attractive in his life, and that was as big a turn-on as how attractive he found Dave.

"Dad, are you daydreaming?" Georgia's voice pulled him out of his thoughts about Dave.

Cam looked around to find all the women in the class looking at him with amusement. He blinked, cleared his throat, and mumbled, "Sorry about that."

They all burst into giggles.

"What put that sloppy grin on your face?" That was from Emma, who was looking mischievously at him.

"Ten to one it's a lady."

"With a look like he had, double or nothing she ain't no *lady*," quipped Kate.

Raucous laughter abounded as Cam felt his cheeks heat, especially when he noticed Georgia laughing along with everyone else.

He managed to weather it well, but as soon as they got into Cam's truck after the class, Georgia dissolved into giggles once more.

"Oh my gosh, Dad. That class! I'm so glad I went with you. I can totally see now why you're taking it."

"Georgia, don't be silly." He concentrated on merging onto the highway.

"Oh, come on, they love you! You're a ladies' man!"

Why was she saying that? As though he wasn't allowed to learn embroidery because he wanted to, that there not only had to be some misguided sexual undertone to her teasing, but it also equated masculine heterosexuality with being a predator. As though he were infiltrating women's spaces for the sole purpose of *getting some*.

"I'm taking this class because I like it." He didn't say the rest. He was too busy trying to figure out where she'd learned that way of thinking. He should be allowed to take a class without any ulterior motive just because it was "for girls."

"And pretty Miss Jenny Lynn has nothing to do with it, huh?" Georgia was laughing.

He usually loved it when Georgia laughed. It mattered to him that his daughter was happy and could live with such a carefree attitude. But this was different.

Sure, Georgia had a point: Jenny Lynn *was* pretty. Anyone could see that.

But Jenny Lynn didn't have an elegant penis, and even if she did, his attraction lay more around a smooth, flat chest, broad shoulders, narrow hips, long legs dusted with coarse black hair, and the deep register of male grunts.

Cam shook his head. "I like her. She's a good teacher, but . . ." He wasn't sure what to say that wouldn't make an even worse liar out of him.

Georgia sighed. "Dad. It would be okay, you know that? If you wanted to date someone. I wouldn't be upset." She'd grown serious.

Did she think that was what was holding him back from asking out Jenny Lynn? The fear of hurting his children by dating someone who wasn't their mother?

Because he'd already gone past that point.

Georgia continued, "I mean, it would probably be weird at first. I should be honest about that. I don't think I'd like it as much as I say I would. But I'd get over it, especially if it meant you could move on."

That startled him. "You think I haven't moved on?" That surprised him so much he almost missed the exit for his apartment. He flipped on his signal and quickly changed lanes.

"I don't know. Ever since Mom died, you've been different." Georgia let out a mirthless laugh. "Not like I'm saying you should have celebrated or anything. But you're different."

And here he thought he'd gotten away with not showing the turmoil of this new phase in his life.

They rolled to a stop at the light at the end of the access road. Cam turned to look at her. "Georgia, I do really appreciate how much you care. If I ever decide to ask out a woman, I promise I will tell you as soon as it happens, okay?"

That much was true. But it wasn't the whole truth.

She nodded. "I'm sorry, Dad," she whispered.

He hated deceiving her. *Hated* it.

"It's fine. I promise. You have nothing to apologize for."

While he had so much to regret.

By the time Georgia drove out of his complex on Sunday morning, Cam was no longer sure who he was or what his place in life should be. His emotions were ragged enough that when Dave phoned and invited him over to "catch up," Cam was out the door and starting up his truck before they hung up the call.

When he rolled up Dave's driveway barely twenty minutes later, Dave was already outside to meet him with a kiss.

"I missed you." Dave murmured the words as he nuzzled Cam's neck.

"I—*oh*—missed you—*mmm*—too."

They stayed like that until Cam felt his mind clearing and his muscles relaxing, plus a little longer, until Dave finally pulled away, and they walked inside. Cam half expected to be immediately led into Dave's bedroom after a greeting like that, but instead they ended up on the back patio with a bottle of wine between them, sitting in wide lounge chairs looking out over the hills.

"It's a beautiful view," Cam said, marveling at how the late-afternoon sun turned the landscape almost gold.

"I like it." Dave took a sip of wine. "Actually, I love it. This view is one of the reasons I bought the house."

"Think you'll stay in Austin forever?" Cam was suddenly, urgently curious.

"Forever is a long time." Dave leaned back in his chair and stretched out his long legs. Cam felt a surge of arousal at the sight. The man even had beautiful feet, for goodness' sake.

"I'd like to stay as long as I can, though," Dave continued. "I like it here. I tell people that the Northeast is my home, but the reality is I feel like I really *belong* in Texas." He snorted. "Well, Austin, anyway. I wouldn't want to be gay anywhere else in this state."

Cam could certainly agree with that.

"So, how was the rest of Georgia's visit?" Dave reached over and took Cam's hand, holding it between their chairs.

They'd texted regularly, but the last time they'd spoken over the phone had been Friday night, when Georgia had gone out with Maisey and Emma from the embroidery class, after all, and Cam had waited up for her at home, fretting as the clock started creeping past midnight with no word from Georgia.

"It was real nice. It's always nice to see my kids."

"But?" Dave prompted.

Cam huffed. Of course Dave would know there was a *but* in there. There was no use pretending otherwise, either. He *wanted* to tell Dave.

"But she's not a child anymore, and I didn't truly realize it until this week. She's talking about interviews and internships and things I know nothing about. I can't help her with any of it. She goes out to clubs and bars and talks about how annoying it is that men keep buying her drinks when she's just trying to have fun with her friends." He sighed. "Between Georgia blazing her own trail and Elijah telling me he doesn't want to inherit the business, I'm feeling . . ." He found himself at a loss for the right word.

Dave's fingers squeezed around his. "I understand."

Well, that made one of them.

Cam looked over at Dave. "Did you ever want kids?"

"I did."

"Really?"

Dave laughed. "You were expecting me to say no?"

Cam flushed. "Yeah, I guess so. I'm sorry."

Dave gestured with his wineglass as if to say, *Doesn't matter.* "I think if I met me now, I'd assume the same thing." He turned to stare out at the landscape. "But yeah, once upon a time it was something I wanted. But my ex . . ." He stopped for a second, then shook his head. "Well, let's just say I'm glad it never worked out, and over time I got used to a life without children."

"Do you ever regret it?"

Cam knew he was being too obvious, but Dave simply looked back at him for a long moment before answering, "Of course I do. But it was the choice I made, and I'm at peace with it. I don't want to spend my life atoning for something that was never really a sin in the first place."

LaVerne used to say something similar: that regrets awarded much more wisdom and foresight to our past selves than what we could have possibly been capable of possessing at the time.

He nodded. "My wife used to—" But he stopped himself abruptly. He'd said it before: LaVerne had no place in this part of his life.

Dave was quiet for a bit before stroking up Cam's arm and rubbing his shoulder. "It's okay to talk about her, you know."

Cam looked to the side. "But I'd rather not."

Dave sighed. "Fair enough."

Cam was pretty sure Dave was thinking of how he'd cut himself off right before he'd been about to say something about his ex. Even though it made Cam feel uneasy that Dave had thoughts of his own that he preferred to keep private, it was good to know that Dave understood the reluctance Cam was experiencing.

"How was your ride with the guys yesterday? Is Richard's knee better?" Cam asked, not wanting to give either of them time to dwell on the exchange they'd just had.

"He's improving, but he sat out yesterday's ride. He met us at the café afterward and seemed pretty pissed off about it. I admit, I also prefer when he's riding with us, because when it's just me and Pedro, we get really competitive. I'm pretty sore today." He laughed. "Richard accused us of acting like children."

Cam laughed too. "I guess none of us ever really grow up. Maybe I'll get in better shape so I can join you guys."

Dave blew a raspberry at him. "You're in great shape." His voice dipped low, and for a second, he gave Cam a come-hither look before grinning and adding, "Don't do it for my sake, anyway. I'd rather you do what you love and enjoy it than do something that you don't really like just to appease me—or anyone."

Cam leaned over the armrest. "Maybe I won't get in better shape, then."

"I have a few other suggestions for how you could work up a sweat, though," Dave murmured.

This time, when they went into the house, they did fall onto that big, soft couch, where Dave worked his magic mouth on Cam's body before Cam paid him back with gusto.

Afterward, as they lay naked in each other's arms, Cam thought about Dave's words.

"Do what you love and enjoy it . . . something that you don't really like just to appease . . ."

But some things were easier said than done. Especially things that he already knew would lead to regret.

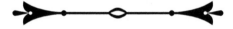

1997

"What a beautiful little princess!"

Hannah Clark was cooing over Georgia, whom LaVerne had dressed in some massive frilly concoction of lace and ruffles and shiny bits. A small group of women had gathered in the living room, standing over Cam's daughter and exclaiming over the one-year-old, who was celebrating her birthday that day.

Or, rather, everyone *else* was celebrating Georgia's first while Georgia herself was trying to rip that ugly dress off, to no avail.

LaVerne's mom beamed with pride as she nodded in agreement. "In another few years, she'll already be giving her daddy a run for his money. He'll have to fend off the boys with a shotgun."

Cam cringed at the conversation.

"Oh, I can believe it," his mom replied. "Look at Elijah. Already a little ladies' man. He's got a few girlfriends in his kindergarten class who are always trying to steal kisses."

"That's my grandson," LaVerne's dad piped in.

Cam had to turn around and walk back into the kitchen to keep from shouting at them. Elijah was hardly five years old. He wasn't a ladies' man. He wasn't even a gentlemen's man. Not yet, no matter whom he preferred. And, for God's sake, Georgia had barely just learned to walk. She certainly didn't need him to be fending off boys. Besides, he hoped when the time came to make choices like that, she'd be able to "fend off" anyone all on her own.

Princess. Ladies' man.

No.

They were children. Small and sweet and smelling like sunshine and innocence.

"Cam was the same way. All the girls loved him," he heard Mom say as he left the room.

And look how that turned out.

He supposed he could take solace in the fact that their words didn't actually *mean* anything, but he hated all the expectations that their words created in the minds of these children. In all their minds. The assumptions and stereotypes that became unspoken, unwritten rules. Rules that could ruin a person if they were ever broken.

June Baxter was a prime example. The older generation had made the same statements about her—Cam remembered being a newlywed when she was a toddler and he'd heard the talk about how beautiful she was, how she'd grow up to turn heads. Titus Fogg, one year older than June, had been labeled a heartbreaker.

When the news got out six months ago that June was pregnant by Titus and he'd refused to marry her, those unspoken rules had kicked in, and June had been ostracized.

Meanwhile, Titus wasn't completely immune. He got frowned at plenty. Mothers of good girls kept their daughters away from him. But most still greeted him in town, even if not with warm enthusiasm. He didn't get fired from his job at the grocery store, either.

Cam knew that, in time, Titus would be accepted back into everyday life in Bitter and his life would go on. June had been forced to move away and was now living with an aunt in Laredo.

Everyone knew she'd never be back.

He understood why they did it. They were a vulnerable enough population already, and everyone worked hard to make sure their community fell in line. Marching to the same beat meant unity, solidarity, *safety*. When you all shared the same views and values, there'd never be a question of whether you'd be willing to fight for what was important.

And there was never any question of what was important.

Princess. Ladies' man. Head turner. Heartbreaker.

Not if he could help it. He might not be able to stop others from saying those things, but he could sure as hell do his best to teach Elijah and Georgia not to bend to the silly labels of conformists. That even if the rest of the town didn't agree with them, his children should have nothing to fear because *Cam* would be their safety.

And maybe, if he did it right, they'd have something he'd never had: the courage to walk away from that safety and risk their own path.

Chapter Thirteen

C am went home on Sunday night. Dave again welcomed him to sleep over, but Cam refused once more. *I'm not ready*, he'd said, as honest as he could be, and Dave accepted his refusal without protest.

It was one of the many reasons why he liked Dave so much. And the same reason why he was so afraid of getting more deeply involved. Yet he couldn't stay away. Dave wasn't just a means to an end, Cam knew it. Dave wasn't an anonymous hookup simply for the sake of saying that Cam knew what it was like to be with a man.

Dave was a way of life.

One that Cam didn't have the capacity to live.

On Wednesday, Cam took Dave out to dinner, then back to his apartment. They ended up on Cam's bed, hands and mouths bringing one another to pleasure.

That night, Dave slept over, though it was mostly because they were both simply exhausted after their respective orgasms and fell asleep in the warm comfort of their embrace.

When Dave shot out of bed at five in the morning, rapid-fire mumbling about being late for work, Cam happily took up the reins of being the calming, soothing presence. He made Dave coffee in a travel mug and sent him out the door with a lingering kiss and a promise that everything would be okay.

Somehow, in some strange way, that was the moment that things began to change. Cam no longer felt like the weaker man in their dynamic—hadn't even *realized* he'd felt that way until he closed the door behind Dave.

He was ready.

When Cam rolled into Dave's driveway on Friday evening, it was almost as though he already knew what would happen tonight. This wasn't the long, fumbling courtship of his teenage years or the casual-hookups-turned-serious relationships that Elijah had said was the most common approach amongst his friends.

He knew what it wasn't. And, yet, he wasn't quite sure what it *was*.

Cam made it through dinner without feeling too nervous. He even managed to initiate making out with Dave after dessert. But when Dave took him by the hand and wordlessly led him to the bedroom, to the sumptuous, down-quilt-covered mattress and tufted velvet headboard, it was difficult to muster the courage to be an adult about it.

"I'm nervous about this," he admitted between kisses.

To Dave's credit, he didn't pretend not to understand. "We can wait, if you want. We have time."

No, we don't.

Cam shook his head. "I don't want to wait. I just had to say it."

Dave gave a soft laugh. "Okay." He stroked a hand over Cam's head and gripped him lightly around the back of the neck, a gently possessive gesture that shot a bolt of arousal straight between Cam's legs.

At Cam's sharp inhale, Dave murmured, "Do you like that?"

"Yes." It came out in a half groan.

"What else do you like?"

Cam wracked his brain for an answer. He liked everything he'd done with Dave, but he wasn't exactly brimming over with specifics.

He must have looked as bewildered as he felt, because Dave asked a different question, instead.

"What about fantasies? Do you ever think about things you haven't tried yet?"

Cam could feel the heat in his cheeks as he nodded. "Yes." He swallowed, hard. "I think about being on my back with you—" that last word came out on a puff of air "—inside me."

Dave groaned, and that low, needy sound, combined with the sudden press of hips against Cam's, left Cam in no doubt as to how Dave felt about Cam's fantasy.

He arched back, rubbing against Dave's body as their tongues tangled in a frenzied kiss.

After a long moment, Dave yanked his mouth away, panting. "Are you sure?"

The growling intent in his question made Cam shiver, and breathing became almost painful because his lungs were seizing so forcefully with arousal. "Yes," he wheezed, nodding for added emphasis.

"Thank God."

With those fervently uttered words, Dave took Cam's mouth once more, kissing him hungrily as he walked Cam backward toward the bed. It was a clumsy, noses-knocking, limbs-akimbo maneuver, but it was everything Cam would have wished for.

When the back of Cam's legs hit the mattress, Dave stopped, stepping back to pull Cam's shirt off. His hands smoothed down Cam's chest, fingernails scratching lightly along the trail of hair that led to the button of Cam's jeans.

In three swift movements—*unbutton, unzip, push*—Cam was completely naked, moaning as Dave stroked his cock with barely there pressure, just enough to drive him crazy with wanting *more*. Cam reached out to undress Dave too, but instead found himself being urged to lie back on the mattress. Dave moved to stand between his legs, which dangled over the edge of the bed.

Cam brought his hands up, delving beneath the hem of Dave's shirt, while his legs pushed together, the soft bare skin of his inner thighs rubbing against the rough denim of Dave's jeans.

Dave's hand was still on Cam's shaft, still moving in too-soft, too-slow strokes.

"*More*," Cam moaned, pressing his fingertips into Dave's lower belly as his hips bucked up into the circle of Dave's fingers.

Yes.

But before he could thrust again, Dave removed his hand, and Cam nearly roared with frustration. He didn't manage to get out a sound, though, because Dave leaned down, bracing his hands on either side of Cam's head, and brought their lips together in a full-body kiss that left Cam reeling. The fabric of Dave's clothes, the smell of his skin, the arousal Cam could taste on his tongue . . .

"Please," Cam begged, slurring the word against Dave's lips in the middle of a wet, hot kiss. "I need you."

This time, Dave didn't tease. He straightened, stripped off his clothes, and for a moment simply stood there, staring down at Cam with fire in his gaze.

The sight of such a beautiful man, fully aroused, looming over Cam with so much sexual intent, was too much for Cam to bear. He had to close his eyes to try to get control over his libido. As much as he wanted Dave to rush, to *fill me already!*, he knew it would be better to take it slow.

Just as Dave had promised weeks ago.

Cam opened his eyes again at the sound of a drawer sliding open. Dave was leaning over to reach the intricately carved nightstand, pulling out a small bottle of clear liquid from the drawer that he uncapped before upturning it into his palm.

This time, when he bent over for another deep kiss, Dave brought his hand to Cam's shaft, slicking it up and down several times before he poured more liquid into his palm and dropped his hand lower, spreading the lubricant as he went. Cam felt him explore the soft, sensitive skin behind Cam's testicles, then dip farther down until the tip of his index finger stroked over the tightly furled skin around Cam's opening, enticing a deep, unfettered groan.

"Do you like that?" Dave asked on another stroke, this time finished off with a light pressure, and Cam found himself relaxing into the increasingly familiar touch. Dave must have felt the release of tension too, because a second later, the hot slide of Dave's finger breaching his body had Cam tightening in surprise. He let out a keening sound of part pleasure, part discomfort, and Dave stilled.

"Are you okay?"

Cam nodded, but could feel his ring of inner muscles clenching too hard around the intrusion.

His finger still in Cam's body, Dave dipped down for another long kiss. This time, he was gentle but insistent, plying his mouth against Cam's for what felt like several minutes. By the time he stood up again, his finger had slipped deeper. This time, at the realization, Cam felt himself letting go even more.

And when Dave brought his free hand to massage around the ridged skin of Cam's scrotum, the resultant sensations were unbelievably pleasurable.

"*Oh.*"

At Cam's breathy moan, Dave pushed deeper with his finger while he stroked up with his other hand, a gentle brush up Cam's cock before bringing his palm against Cam's lower belly, rubbing over the skin with soothing strokes, sliding over the tops of Cam's thighs.

"*Mmm.*" He sighed, letting go of the last bit of tension he could feel, and Dave's finger began to stroke.

All the while, Dave kept his eyes riveted on Cam's face. "Is that okay?"

This time, Cam wasn't shy. "*Yes,*" he groaned. "It's more than okay."

Dave grinned, that flash of straight white that Cam adored. "Can you take more?"

"Yes. Give it to me."

Dave brought the bottle of lube between Cam's legs, dripping some down out of sight, then flipped the cap closed and tossed it onto the bed near Cam's waist. A second later, Cam felt the press of another finger at his opening, trying to gain entrance. He let out a breath, and this time the burn of being breached was still a bit painful, but not surprising. Within a couple of more minutes, Dave's two fingers were moving inside of him, each stroke ending with a gentle nudge against a spot in Cam's body that had him nearly insensate.

So good.

He looked up at Dave, wishing he was capable at the moment of doing more than just *lying* there, but the sensations were too overwhelming in their newness.

He wanted more.

"Dave," he panted, "I'm ready."

He hoped that was all he needed to say. Anything more specific—more explicit . . . he wasn't ready for *that.*

Luckily, Dave understood. He nodded, then slowly withdrew his fingers, making Cam shudder and grunt at the loss. Dave leaned far to the right, pushing Cam's leg out as he reached for the top drawer of the nightstand next to the bed.

Cam felt a twinge of pain and let out a breathy laugh, causing Dave to pause and look back at him with a raised brow and a lopsided smile—a silent question.

"I don't think I've been able to stretch my leg this far since I was a kid," he explained. "Although I'm not sure I can actually do it now, to be honest. I have a feeling I'm gonna need some liniment later."

Dave let out a bark of laughter, and Cam felt something jostle up against the physical pleasure that was still humming in his body.

Joy. Care. Something a lot like love . . .

"I'll take care of you," Dave told him with a wink, then slid open the drawer and pulled out a condom packet.

Oh.

This was really happening.

Dave tore open the foil and pulled out the latex ring before tossing the empty packet to the floor. Cam watched it flutter downward and swallowed hard.

Dave set the condom on the engorged head of his cock and slowly—*torturously* slowly, almost—rolled it on, his concentration on the task so complete that Cam couldn't help but find the intensity erotic. He'd been on the receiving end of that focus, and it was heady to watch it from another angle.

When Dave finally brought his fingers in a tight circle around the base of his shaft, Cam moaned. "*Dave.*"

Another kiss, this time with Dave's cock rubbing alongside Cam's as he lay prostrate over Cam's body, had Cam gasping for *more, more, more, please more.*

Dave slowly slid away from Cam's body, picked up the lubricant, and drizzled a long, thin stream of it over his own cock.

Cam whimpered, the only thought in his mind that he'd never seen anything more arousing.

But then Dave dropped the bottle and again gripped the base of his own cock with one hand while smearing the fluid over the head and shaft with the other, and Cam's brain practically short-circuited.

This was the most arousing thing he'd ever seen.

And he had a feeling even that image was about to be obliterated.

Once Dave's erection was fully coated in lubricant, latex glistening as Cam's cock throbbed in response, he gently pushed Cam's right thigh up until Cam's foot was resting on the mattress, then did the same with Cam's left leg.

He felt exposed, awkward, and needy all at once.

And then the tip of Dave's cock was pressing against the place where his fingers had been before, and he leaned in, pressing Cam's knees to spread him open, urging Cam to help him.

"That's it. Yes." Dave pushed forward, the head entering Cam in one slow, continuous movement.

Cam grabbed the backs of his thighs and pulled them up, allowing Dave to go a little deeper. There was a slight pain, but the discomfort was minimal when compared with the incredibly *good* sensations he was experiencing.

And a part of him couldn't believe that, after decades of *wanting*, this was actually happening.

Dave thrust again, and again, and after a few more incremental advances, Cam felt the tickling sensation of wiry hairs brushing against his skin. Another thrust and Dave would probably be bottomed out inside him.

Cam moaned at the thought, pulsing around the hard ridge inside his body, which in turn drew a harsh grunt from Dave.

"You all right?" Dave gritted out the question through a jaw set tight, the cords of his neck standing out against his skin.

Beautiful.

Cam nodded, the back of his head scraping again the duvet, a sound that only emphasized how real, and yet how extraordinary this experience was. "It feels— *You* feel amazing," he breathed, earning a nerve-melting smile from Dave, who then began to move, hips gently pulling back before nudging forward once more.

Cam felt the friction like a shock to his system. He was already harder than he could remember being, the entire top half of his erection had gone purple, it was so flush with blood. Fluid was leaking from the tip at an alarming rate, and from the way Dave licked his lips when he caught sight of the glistening head, they were both more than a little turned on.

Dave braced himself with one hand on Cam's right knee and brought his other hand to wrap around Cam's shaft, beginning to shuttle his hand up and down in firm strokes.

"Oh. *Yes*," Cam hissed.

Dave sank deeper with a groan, hitting that spot in Cam that made him whimper with intense pleasure.

"I'm sorry. Cam. God. I'm not gonna last," Dave told him, already moving faster, pulling out with longer strokes and pushing in with deeper ones, breathing hard, grunting and sweating and—

"I'm *coming*," Cam keened, no longer caring about anything except the seize of his balls, the jerk and shudder of his cock. His orgasm ripped through every muscle in his body, fluid shooting out of him in unbelievably forceful spurts. Dave thrust fast and shallow, once, twice, before he gave a loud, long groan, and Cam felt the pulse of Dave's climax deep inside.

They rode out their orgasms for several long moments, slowly winding down. Dave started to soften and pulled out, making Cam sigh and wince. But when Dave returned to him after a quick cleanup in the bathroom and lay down next to him, arms wrapped around Cam's body as they shared kisses and soft caresses, any lingering memory of pain dissipated, leaving a feeling of fullness that he feared had everything to do with the man in whose arms he rested.

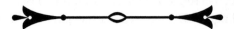

Cam awoke early the next morning, stretching in Dave's luxurious bed. At some point, they had moved beneath the sheets, but otherwise Cam had slept like the dead.

Fitting, he supposed, since this morning he felt like he'd been reborn.

Now you know.

And, yet, he found much less satisfaction in the idea of a question resolved—what it was like to truly be with another man—than he did in how *right* he felt as a result.

Somewhere along the way, what had felt natural but not easy had become . . .

Easy.

What that meant for the future, though . . .

Well, he didn't want to think about that right now. It was still too far away to contemplate.

He ignored the part of his conscience that accused him of avoiding unpleasant truths, and as quietly as possible, slid from the bed to make his way to the bathroom. He brushed his teeth using the toothbrush he'd started keeping in Dave's house and splashed water on his face, blotting it off with a towel in front of the mirror.

His reflection caught his eye, and he lowered the towel to find himself staring in frank perusal at his own face. There were the fine lines at the corners of his eyes, the slight graying at his temples. His jowls had started to droop, not so much that most would notice, but enough that those who had known him at twenty-four would see the difference in his fifty-four-year-old jawline.

It wasn't the face of a model or a movie star. He looked *normal*, he knew. Just like Dave was normal looking. But the wisdom of age, the tempering of time, was something that Cam found impossibly sexy in Dave.

He wanted to think Dave saw the same things in him. But, at the same time, Cam knew how naïve he was, almost like a child. Dave had been so patient with him so far, and even though Dave had never made him feel like he was foolish or immature, it was difficult to realize how very out of his depth he still was.

He didn't know how to reconcile this new uncertainty with the life he'd lived before Dave, in which he'd accepted his fate and strode confidently toward the end of an unexciting, but nonetheless productive existence.

A soft knock on the bathroom door made him jump and tear his gaze away from the mirror.

"Just saying good morning." Dave's voice was muffled through the door.

Cam opened it in a hurry and smiled at Dave's bed-rumpled appearance. "I didn't mean to wake you."

"You didn't." Dave stepped forward and dropped a light kiss on Cam's lips. "The alarm just went off. I have to meet the guys for our ride pretty soon. Richard's knee is mostly healed and he's eager to do this one together. I don't think I can skip it."

Ah, right. It was Saturday morning. Cam felt slightly disappointed that Dave was leaving him so soon, but he couldn't find fault in Dave's choice to be there for his friend. Cam would have done the same thing.

Besides, he still planned to meet the group at the café, and in the meantime it would be good to have a little time alone, to process everything that had happened between them.

He supposed age was useful when it came to having some perspective.

He only wished he could have reached this point without feeling like he'd started over, smack dab in the middle.

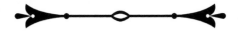

1999

"Well, Mrs. McGhee, the results indicate that you seem to be holding steady. The percentage of sickle cells hasn't increased since your last test, and there are no obvious changes in the health of your internal organs."

LaVerne broke down in tears at the news, that Cam assumed—*hoped*, anyway—were tears of relief.

"D-does that mean I'm okay?" LaVerne sobbed around her question.

Dr. Phillips didn't immediately answer, and when he did, he looked haggard. "It means that you're not declining as quickly as most of the other sickle cell patients we see. It holds with what you've seen in the first thirty years of your life, as well. You've already beaten the odds."

The doctor had matured over the past couple of years, and Cam's respect for the young physician had grown significantly with every visit they paid to his practice. Cam had also gotten to know Dr. Phillips's personality and approach much better too. And, based on the way the doctor was talking, Cam believed that LaVerne wasn't at risk of death . . . for now. But beating the odds in this case still didn't feel like *winning*.

"How quick a decline are we looking at, Doctor?" Cam asked, trying to keep things as gentle as possible, but neither did he want to dance around the topic. They needed to know.

Dr. Phillips gave a small shrug. "I honestly can't say for sure." He looked at LaVerne. "As long as you continue eating right, no drinking or smoking, and don't plan to have any more children—"

LaVerne gasped. "No more babies?"

"I strongly advise against it." Dr. Phillips didn't hesitate. "In fact, my advice to you would be to make sure you have your support systems and end-of-life plans in place and to be constantly evaluating them for fit and practicality."

His voice was soft and slow as he spoke, but the message was too brutally devastating to do anything but leave LaVerne looking stunned.

"I'm sorry, Mrs. McGhee. The results I have here mean *good news*. Today's visit is about celebrating how your condition hasn't changed. I didn't intend—"

Cam cut him off. "We needed to know." He turned to LaVerne. "It's going to be okay. I know it's not easy to hear that there won't be more kids, but we've got two beautiful ones already, right?"

She gulped in a breath, swallowing another sob, and nodded.

"And Dr. Phillips says your condition is unchanged, which means you have time. More time than a lot of others with this disease. Right?"

Another nod.

"So like the doc says, this is something to celebrate. We've gotta make the best of the time we've got. All of us do." He swallowed, eating up the desire to scream at himself for being the last person qualified to give advice like that. "Right?"

LaVerne brought two watery eyes to his, and the pain in her gaze nearly ripped him apart.

"Right," she whispered.

But both of them knew they wouldn't be able to ignore the shadow of what loomed ahead.

Chapter Fourteen

In the car on the way home from Dave's, Cam thought about what had happened the night before and wondered whether the guys would be able to tell. Earlier, he'd thought of Richard and Pedro as Dave's friends, but he realized as he drove that they were his friends now, too.

It sounded stupid when he really *thought* about it, but he hadn't expected to make friends during his time in Austin. Not just with Richard and Pedro, either. There were also the women in the embroidery group. He considered them at least close acquaintances.

The phone rang just as Cam pulled into his apartment complex parking lot for a quick shower and change of clothes before going on to the café. He quickly maneuvered the truck into a spot and answered the call.

"Good morning, Elijah."

He had to admit, having a cell phone with caller ID was pretty nice, though he still sometimes forgot to charge the thing and ended up with a dead device for a few hours on end.

"Hey, Dad. How are you?"

Amazing. Wonderful. A new man.

"I'm all right." He got out of the truck and started heading up the stairs to his door. "You doing okay? How's everything holding up out there?"

"I'm okay too. So's the store. But I wanted to talk to you about it." Elijah sounded serious.

"What's going on? Problem with the new inventory systems?"

"No, nothing like that. It's all going great, actually. We're up by twelve percent over last year and that's after only two weeks of being fully up and running. Even when we'd installed only the point-of-sale systems we were already up by eight."

Cam could hear the pride in Elijah's voice, and his own heart swelled in agreement. His son was a smart man. A numbers man. Sometimes Cam lamented the fact that he'd never pushed Elijah to apply to a famous school. Probably could have gotten a scholarship.

You did the best with what you had at the time. So did he. And look at him now.

"That's real impressive, Elijah. I can't tell you how much I appreciate all you've done."

Did the best with what you had . . .

He'd done the same thing, in a sense. But his story was different. He didn't have his whole life ahead of him anymore.

"Thanks, Dad. But, listen, I was calling to see if you'd gotten in touch with that guy yet. About selling the business?"

Cam unlocked his apartment door and stepped inside. Through the cutout window that allowed him to see directly into the kitchen, his eyes immediately locked on the jar where he'd dropped the contact info for the buyer.

"Uh, not yet. I haven't had a chance."

There was a long pause, as though Elijah knew he was lying and was waiting for Cam to come clean. But Cam wasn't ready to come down off his high from last night. Serious conversations would have to wait.

He shut the door behind him and locked it, kicked off his shoes, and went into the bedroom to pull out some clean clothes.

Finally, Elijah spoke. "What have you been getting up to in Austin? Georgia was going on about how *happy* you seem."

Getting up to. As though he were making mischief of some sort.

He snorted. *Kids.* Sometimes they were too smart for their own good. At least Georgia seemed to approve of his life here.

"Oh, you know. The same old. We talked about this."

"Georgia said you're taking embroidery."

Elijah's tone put Cam on edge. "I am." He wondered if she'd told Elijah what he'd been embroidering.

Another long pause, and Cam grabbed his change of clothes and padded into the bathroom. Just when he was about to tell Elijah he had to get off the phone, his son found his voice once again.

"I'm glad you're happy."

Cam stopped, standing in socked feet on the cold tile floor, and closed his eyes.

Kids.

He couldn't imagine life without them.

"Thank you, Elijah. I— Thank you."

It was the only thing worth saying. He'd spent so many years without the freedom to be fully happy, that gratitude for Elijah's approval—because his son's approval *mattered*, whether he wanted it to or not—was all he could feel right now.

"Don't mention it." Elijah sounded uncomfortable now, and Cam twisted his lips in a wry grin. Despite his best efforts, Elijah had fallen victim to the larger expectations of men, and he wasn't great with expressing his feelings. Better than Cam ever had been. Better than a lot of other men.

It was difficult not to want better for his own child, though. But it was too late. Elijah was an adult now.

It's never too late.

"If you get a chance to call that guy, let me know, okay? I'm curious to hear what he says."

Elijah had deftly switched topics, and Cam found himself nodding. "Will do."

They said their good-byes, and Cam ended the call, then set the phone on the sink top.

"I'm glad you're happy."

And he was. Georgia was right. Cam was happy, fully and completely.

But how long would it last?

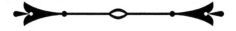

It was finished.

Cam tied off the last thread in back of the canvas and clipped it.

Jenny Lynn walked by at that moment and clapped her hands together in excitement. "You've finished!"

There was a chorus of gasps and shuffling movement as the women in the class stood, craned, and twisted to see Cam's completed embroidery project. Jenny Lynn held out her hands. "May I show everyone?"

He suddenly felt wildly vulnerable, which he knew was silly, because they'd all seen one another's projects over the past few weeks. Everyone already knew what he'd been working on. Showing them the completed version shouldn't be a big deal.

But it felt monumental.

Jenny Lynn was waiting.

Taking a deep breath, he nodded . . . and placed the Aida into her hands.

When she held it up, the class *oohed* and *ahhed* with fervor.

"It's beautiful, Cam," gushed Kate. "I wish I'd chosen that word." She immediately giggled at herself. "Ha, *chosen*."

He smiled. His canvas was done up in shades of green, because it was his favorite color. Green lines, green dots, green swirls. And in the middle of it all, in bright yellow, like an ear of corn poking out from the leaves: *Choices*.

His word.

His life.

But not because he'd had so many throughout his time on Earth. In fact, his life had been strangely *devoid* of choices.

Until now.

And he found himself yearning with a strange nostalgia for a time when things were so much more clear.

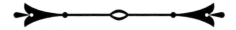

2009

That Tuesday was the first time Cam had ever closed the shop on a weekday.

But the entire town of Bitter had shut down for good reason. At least a hundred people were crowded into Ruth Ann's Restaurant on Main Street, eyes glued to the large television behind the serving counter.

Ruth Ann's was technically closed too. They weren't serving food, anyway. But the place had the biggest TV in town, and most folks wanted to get together in celebratory honor of this moment.

Standing next to him, pressed up against their friends and neighbors, he felt LaVerne squeeze his hand when the newly sworn-in president concluded his inaugural address.

"Oh, Cam," she sighed. "I can't . . . I'm so grateful that I've lived to see this."

He could hear tears in her voice. He turned to look at her, saw the sheen of moisture in her eyes.

"LaVerne—" He wanted to tell her that he felt the same way, but her truth had such a deeper layer to it that he was glad when she cut him off before he could utter the words that would diminish her pain.

"No. Cam. I can feel the difference every year. I'm more tired, more worn out. I don't know how much longer I have left. It's time to start facing up to the probability that I'm not going to be around for many more years, and this . . ." She shook her head slowly.

"It's something very special," Cam said quietly.

"It makes me think about all the choices I've made in my life and how much more is available to people like us—to *me*—since the year I was born, and I feel a little sad." She made a small sound of dismay. "Cam. I'm sorry. I wasn't trying to say that I regret—"

"I understand, LaVerne." He didn't want to hear what she had to say next. It might make him do something horrible, like walk away from everything and never look back.

LaVerne looked at him intently. "Times have changed, haven't they?"

Did she know? Had she guessed the truth of who he was?

He gaped at her.

"Sometimes the change of times changes who we are too. Changes what we want." She gave a sad laugh. "Although I wouldn't want you to make any big changes until *after* I'm gone."

She *had* to know.

Maybe.

If she didn't, though, he couldn't say anything, because then . . . then *she'd know*.

Besides, she might be right in the general sense, but time hadn't opened up any more choices for him. At least, not here in Bitter. This was the way life was and always would be. The only choice he had was to accept the life he'd made and make the most of what he had.

Chapter Fifteen

"Remember that offer to buy the feed business?"

Cam was lying next to Dave in his bed, holding their entwined hands up to stare at the interlacing of their fingers. Two shades of brown in their strong, broad palms pressed together.

Dave hummed. "Yeah, I do. I was wondering about that. Figured you'd tell me when you decided something."

Cam gave a quiet laugh. "I did finally call the man yesterday."

Was it just him, or had Dave tensed up?

"I got the details," Cam continued. "And it's a good offer. A really good one."

"Oh?" Dave let go of Cam's hand and rolled toward him. Cam did the same so that they were face to face.

"Yeah. I could retire as long as I kept my costs down. Bitter isn't exactly an expensive place to live."

Dave's expression grew tight. "You'd stay in Bitter?"

"I don't know yet. I don't even know if I'll sell."

"Do you want to?"

Cam sighed. "I don't know that, either. I never believed I'd even *have* a choice like this. I don't—"

"Do you miss running the business?"

"No," Cam admitted.

"Well, then, what's keeping you from selling?"

The tone of Dave's voice made Cam bristle a bit, but he tried to keep himself in check, at least long enough to explain.

He had to roll away, though, to look up at the ceiling instead of at Dave. Having that dark, penetrating stare on him made him feel too vulnerable.

"I wish it were that simple." He shook his head against the bed. "I really do. I started the store because I didn't have an education and my parents needed help. The house I live in back in Bitter was the house where my dad grew up. His father had inherited their farm, but through a bunch of bad luck and poor decisions, they lost most of it. By the time I was in high school, there wasn't a whole lot left—just enough to keep my parents going. I had to do something to support my own family, and even though I didn't love the day-to-day of having a feed store, it was the life I *knew*, and I made the most . . ."

All the small throwaway thoughts and big revelations of the past week swirled around in his mind before he finished. "I made the most of what I had."

It all meant something. But he was having a hard time figuring out what. Sell, not sell, stay, go . . .

For the first time in his life, he had choices, and they were overwhelming.

"I understand," Dave said quietly. He reached over and settled his palm directly over Cam's heart.

Dave didn't push for more, but for the first time, Cam wondered if so many unspoken words between them would eventually create a barrier so big that being together would be an impossibility, regardless of how many miles did or didn't separate them.

Cam wanted to close his eyes, curl into a ball, and hide for a while. Instead, he brought his own hand up to cover Dave's. Reuniting.

For now, it was enough.

"Hey." Dave bent his elbow and propped his head up in his free hand, grinning down at Cam. "My niece is having her quinceañera next Saturday night. Want to come with me?"

Dave had told him the story at some point of how his younger sister had come to visit for a summer and ended up meeting her husband during that time. She'd stayed, and now Dave had two nephews and a niece in San Antonio.

Before Cam could answer, Dave added, "No one will care if you're my date, but if it bothers you, then it's fine by me. I can introduce you as my friend, instead."

Then again, maybe that's why Dave wasn't pushing. Maybe Dave was holding back because Cam was.

Cam hesitated, watching Dave's eyes. There was something there, even in the dim light, that felt significant.

"I'd love to come," he said, the words coming slowly as he processed his thoughts. "And I . . ." *Another choice. Another chance.* "I think it's fine if you tell people we're dating."

He hadn't *dated* since he was a teenager. When he'd been with LaVerne.

It made him feel strange.

But then Dave smiled, his face so suffused with joy that Cam forgot anything but the radiance coming from his lover.

Lover.

That didn't make him feel as strange as he might have thought it should.

And, a moment later, when Dave rolled forward to kiss him, he felt absolutely perfect.

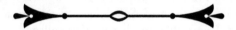

Cam had been at Solea's quinceañera for nearly an hour, and the party had been so intricate that Dave had only just managed to snag his sister for a minute to introduce her to Cam.

Jacqui squealed and grabbed him in a strong hug. "It's so nice to finally meet you, Cam! I've been hearing about you for so long, I feel like our introduction is past due!"

She'd heard about him? And for "so long"?

Cam felt his cheeks heat at the same time he swelled with pride that Dave had been talking about him to her.

"It's nice to meet you too. This is an incredible party. I've never been to a quinceañera."

Jacqui laughed. "I hadn't been to one, either, until I met Nelson and all his family and friends. Back when we were dating, it felt like we went to something like this at least once a month." She grinned. "Actually, it's still like that, but at least now I can understand what's going on instead of wandering around smiling like an idiot and nodding my head at inappropriate times."

Dave piped in. "Jacqui took a few years of Spanish at the community college in order to be able to blend in better with Nelson and his crew. Her accent is still terrible, though."

Jacqui scoffed in mock offense. "Says the man who knows three whole words in Spanish."

Cam turned to Dave. "What are the three words?"

"The three *b*'s: beer, bathroom, and bicycle." Dave grinned when Cam laughed. "Hey, that's all I need to be happy."

"Well, if your happiness lies in *b* words, you need the *four b's*," Jacqui teased. "Because you're a lot happier since your boyfriend came on the scene."

Cam nearly dropped his jaw, but managed to hold back his surprise when he saw Dave looking embarrassed at Jacqui's remarks. He cast about for something else to talk about, and his eyes landed on Dave's niece, standing and laughing with another girl who looked about the same age.

Cam nodded in Solea's direction. "Who is the girl with your daughter? They seem to be joined at the hip."

Jacqui took the cue immediately, glancing over at Solea with a fond, proud look. "Oh, that's Solea's best friend, Erica. They're two peas in a pod. Erica's older brother is off at college and couldn't get back for this, but he and José—did you meet my son?"

Cam nodded.

"Oh, good. So José and Marcus are also quite close. We've all known each other since they were in grade school. Sometimes I can't believe they're so grown-up." Jacqui's face went wistful before she gently shook herself and straightened. "Actually, you should meet Erica's dads. They moved here ten years ago, and they've added so much to our community. Glenn and Roger are practically family." She rose on her tiptoes, looking around the crowded room for a minute before calling out, "Oh, there they are! Come on, I'll introduce you."

Jacqui led them a short distance over to a man who was standing with his back to them, standing in a small circle with another man and an older woman.

Funny. Something about his back was oddly familiar.

It's a back. Nothing more.

But as they got closer, things started to click into place, and Cam found himself tensing.

No. It isn't possible.

At the touch of Jacqui's hand on his shoulder, the man excused himself and started to turn. Cam's heart began to race.

My God. Glenn and—

"Roger, I'd like you to meet—"

"Roger Henderson?"

Cam and Jacqui spoke at the same time, immediately followed by Dave and Jacqui chorusing, "You *know* each other?"

Cam stared at Roger, still trying to process what he was seeing.

A ghost.

Roger was the first to speak. "We're from the same town."

"Oh, Cam, I didn't realize you were from Dallas!" Jacqui exclaimed.

Roger's eyes widened slightly. Given what Cam knew about Roger's history, he gathered that Roger hadn't mentioned Bitter to Jacqui, despite those *ten years of practically family*.

So he nodded instead.

Roger looked relieved.

When Cam nodded in agreement, Dave must have realized something else was going on, because he wrapped an arm around his sister. "Hey, Jacqui, why don't you take me over to the guest of honor and let these guys catch up? I can swing back around later. I've barely had a minute to talk to my favorite niece."

"She's your only niece," Jacqui countered.

"Still my favorite."

Jacqui rolled her eyes but excused both of them, and they sauntered off, leaving Cam alone with Roger and the other man who'd been standing in their small circle. The woman they'd been talking to seemed to have melted away.

"Cam McGhee. Been a long time," Roger ventured.

Cam was still reeling. "Roger. My gosh. I don't— The world can't possibly be this small."

At that, Roger seemed to unwind a little, shoulders relaxing as he snorted. "The world seems impossibly huge when you live in Bitter, but once you leave, you realize just how small it is. But it's good to see you too, anyway."

Cam flushed. "Oh, man. I'm sorry. I . . ." He gave an apologetic shrug, uncertain of what to say.

Roger gave a little cough, reaching out to put a hand on the arm of his companion, a slightly heavyset white man of average height with thinning light-brown hair that didn't quite match his coarse-looking face. But despite the odd combination of features, there was a smiling friendliness about his eyes that turned him into a surprisingly attractive man.

"Cam, this is my husband, Glenn."

"Nice to meet you, Cam." Glenn held out his hand, and Cam shook it almost on autopilot.

It had been over thirty years since he'd seen Roger, but he'd never forgotten the older man. For so long, Roger had been Cam's reminder not to stray out of his comfort zone. Roger had been his warning beacon, his moral of the story.

Roger was married. Had a child—*children*. Roger seemed happy and comfortable and everything Cam believed wouldn't be possible if he'd left Bitter and his lies behind.

"How long have you been with Dave?" Roger asked, smiling politely. It was a simple enough question, but Cam could hear the bigger question underlying it.

Cam found his voice enough to reply, "I— A couple of months. Um, I don't know if you heard, but LaVerne . . . she died just over a year ago."

Roger's face fell into genuine sympathy. "I'm so sorry. She was a good woman." He turned slightly to address Glenn. "LaVerne was Cam's wife." He looked back at Cam. "You were still married?"

Cam nodded. "Thirty-five years." He thought about the assumption Dave had made on their first date and added, "I'm not b-bi." He stumbled over the word, still unused to including it in regular conversation. But his stutter, albeit small, seemed to magnify the impact of what he was saying, because a heavy silence fell between them.

Thirty-five years of denial was a long time.

There had been happiness in there too, though. There was Elijah and Georgia. This unexpected meeting shouldn't—*couldn't*—change that.

"I'm sorry for your loss," Glenn murmured. "I couldn't help but overhear that you're from, uh, not Dallas?"

Cam exchanged a brief look with Roger before replying, "Yes. I came out here a short time ago. My kids were urging me to get out a bit. They were worried, I think."

"Must be hard to be away for so long," Glenn suggested.

Cam hesitated for a moment. *Was* it hard? He'd thought it would be. He sometimes told himself it was. But he wasn't sure now that his assessment was correct.

Because here, there was Dave.

There was freedom.

But he still wasn't sure how to answer. Instead, all he said was, "I, uh, I'm going back to Bitter at the end of July."

"I see." Glenn's lips pursed, and Cam was sure he'd heard every detail about the treatment Roger had suffered at the hands of young men in Bitter.

"Doug Hodgkins and his boys beat Roger down last night."

"His ma found him in the fields this morning . . ."

"We don't recognize that name in our lives any longer."

"I'm sorry," Cam blurted. "Roger, I . . . If I had known, I—"

Would have what? Stopped Doug and that gang and probably gotten beat yourself?

Roger sighed. "It's in the past, Cam. I appreciate it. I do. But I got over it. What happened that night will never be *okay*. But I lived, which was the only thing I'd ever wanted to do anyway. I lived and loved—" he glanced over at Glenn for a moment "—and that's already more than so many others got to do. We adopted two great kids. We got married a week after it was declared legal. We go on family vacations, and we make pancakes on Saturday and squabble about whose turn it is to choose a movie. We are normal people with normal lives, and I treasure every minute of it because I know how close I came to losing it."

Cam's throat felt tight, but he managed to choke out, "I'm glad you didn't."

And then Roger did something Cam hadn't expected, which was probably why he didn't stiffen, but rather sank fully and heavily into the *hug* that Roger gave him.

"You're a good man, Cam. I don't care whom you love as long as you're loving. That's all there is to it." Roger patted him on the back, but a second later broke away at the sound of Jacqui saying his name.

"I'm sorry to interrupt, but Erica wants her purse." Jacqui looked amused, and only then did Cam notice the little bright-purple, rhinestone-studded bag dangling from Glenn's left wrist. The purse was the same color as Erica's fancy gown.

"That girl—" Glenn began.

"Has us wrapped around her little finger," Roger finished.

Glenn nodded, and they both laughed.

Cam found himself feeling oddly jealous.

Roger squeezed Glenn's arm, and the two exchanged a brief glance before Roger said, "I better go find out what Erica's up to. I hope I'll see you again, Cam. Preferably sooner than thirty years from now too."

They walked off with Jacqui toward Erica.

Cam stood there for barely five seconds, reeling and alone, before Dave appeared, as though he'd been watching from afar and had waited for the exact moment when Cam might need him.

"I've been hearing about you for so long . . ."

It hit him, then. Really hit him, how much Dave must care. How much investment had gone into *not* pushing.

Dave wrapped an arm around Cam's shoulder and leaned in close. "You okay?"

"Yeah." His voice came out raspy, but he nodded for emphasis and added in a clearer voice. "I'm good."

Dave frowned at him. "Do you want to go home?"

Cam shook his head. "No, I—" His words caught up with him, and he realized that they were true. If they left, it would feel like running away. And he was tired of running. He had run to Austin, trying to leave behind the questions that plagued him back home. He only had a short time here, and he didn't want to waste it.

"Really, let's stay." He grinned. "I don't want to miss the cake."

He didn't want to miss *anything*.

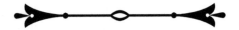

2013

"LaVerne, you can't be serious."

Cam scowled at LaVerne. She was in a wheelchair now, for goodness' sake. There was no way she was going to be riding in the car for the ten hours to Colorado Springs. Not to mention . . .

"We've already talked about how far it is. Think of the elevation too. You might end up struggling to breathe on top of everything else."

She was declining much more quickly than she ever had before. She'd started this year about the same as she had been, but last month she'd developed a lot of leg pain, having to spend a few days in bed, unmoving. Three weeks ago, Dr. Phillips had ordered her into a wheelchair "until she recovered."

They all suspected that day would never come.

"You listen to me, Cam." LaVerne's voice was so full of anger, it was shaking. "I am *not* going to miss my son's graduation. While there is still breath in me, I refuse to ease my own pain over being there for my children. This is a proud moment for him. For me. For *us*. I. Am. Going."

Cam stared at her for a beat. LaVerne rarely insisted on anything. There was no way now that he would fight her on this.

He nodded. "Okay."

"And don't even think about keeping me from going to Dallas in the fall to bring Georgia to SMU." Her expression faltered, and she added in a whisper, "If I'm still around."

Cam immediately knelt and took her hands. "You'll be around, LaVerne. I know you will."

LaVerne didn't look at him, but shrugged gently. "You know, I think you might be right. But this feels like the beginning of the end." She laughed softly. "I think I said that ten years ago too. But, this time, I really mean it. I can *feel* my body breaking down."

"LaVerne . . ." He squeezed her fingers gently. "Are you *sure* you're up to the trip?" He knew she was—he understood that it wasn't every day your eldest graduated from the Air Force Academy—but he had to ask, one last time.

"Cam." She finally met his eyes. "Life has a funny way of showing us who we truly are, simply by the passage of time. Age wears down our bodies, but it brings so much more certainty to our hearts. And what we might not have seen in our youth becomes crystal clear across decades."

Was she still talking about the drive to Colorado?

Cam didn't think so.

But then she huffed and smiled. "A ten-hour drive is a drop in the bucket of that time. I might worsen somewhat because of the trip, but it won't matter. It took me fifty years to get to where I am now. The ten hours I spend in a little discomfort in exchange for the joy and pride and peace that I'll get in return is a bargain deal." She leaned forward slightly, intensifying her gaze. "I'm *sure*."

Well, that makes one of us.

But he didn't say that. Instead, he merely nodded and moved to stand. "I never could say no to you, LaVerne."

That wasn't true, though, and they both knew it. He had a sinking feeling the problem was really that he could never say *yes* to himself.

Chapter Sixteen

D ave took Cam home after the quinceañera, kissed and undressed him like he was something precious, entered him slowly, eyes riveted on Cam's, and caressed and stroked his body inside and out until they were both moaning and shuddering with pleasure.

It was healing, though Cam didn't realize that until the following morning, when he woke up feeling much more solid. He wound himself around Dave's sleep-warmed body and contented himself with where he was in that moment.

After that, life fell into a pattern of sorts. Cam was with Dave three nights a week, always sleeping together in the same bed on those nights regardless of at whose place they ended up; he met the guys at the café on Saturdays; and during the week he read, walked, and picked up a pottery class when the embroidery ended.

Choices hung on the wall in his apartment next to the dining table, a sentinel as time rushed past. The months moved so quickly that Cam was startled one day to find himself at the middle of May, only nine days away from Georgia's graduation.

"Did you book a hotel?" Georgia asked over the phone when she called that morning.

"Yep, I did that a month ago, honey." *With Dave's help.* But he didn't share that. The secret he was keeping from his children was the only blot marring his currently otherwise ideal existence.

Georgia laughed. "Of course you did. You're a phone whiz now. Now that you've mastered using it, you need to get a dating profile."

"No, I don't." Even talking about it felt like a betrayal of what he had with Dave.

"Dad, I know you still miss Mom, but I think it would be good for you."

She still thought he was reticent to date because of LaVerne. Cam grasped for an answer that wouldn't be quite a lie, but also wouldn't upset Georgia. "She was a good woman, Georgia. Your mom loved you very much."

Georgia was quiet, though. *Hmm.* Maybe that hadn't worked as well as he'd hoped.

"Sweetheart—"

"Have you *thought* about dating since she died? Getting remarried, even?"

She threw him off with her question.

He closed his eyes in a long blink, searching for the right thing to say. "I'm okay. Really." *I have Dave.* "But I do appreciate that you—"

"Having a social life is *important*, Dad." Georgia wasn't letting it go. "I learned all about this in my psych class last year."

Lord, deliver me from young adults thinking they're experts after one semester of introductory theory.

She seemed oblivious to his growing anxiety and irritation, though, and pressed on. "Even if it's just to meet new people, you should get on social media. You don't have to be romantically interested in anyone. Embroidery and pottery aren't going to net you what you need."

Don't tell me what I need.

He gritted his teeth and counted to five, then released a long breath. "I'm *all right*. But thank you." He tried to sound as firm as he could without actually scolding. Hopefully that would end her badgering. Tension was starting to climb up his neck.

But she didn't give up. "I *care* about you. I don't want you to be lonely. Maybe there's a widow out there who will understand what you've been through, and you can support one another. It's not healthy to be so alone."

I'm not alone, and even if I were, it's none of your business.

"Georgia." His tone was starting to get sharp. "It's not for me. I don't want to meet someone who—"

"But you might end up finding a woman who loves you as much as Mom loved you. Maybe you can—"

"I don't want a woman. I have a *boyfriend*! *Enough*!" The confession came roaring out before he had a chance to realize what he was saying.

And when abrupt, complete silence fell between them, he immediately wanted to take it all back.

Oh. Lord.

"Georgia," he rasped.

"You—" she immediately started, as though his voice had snapped her into action, but then she stopped abruptly before restarting. "How long—" Another pause, then finally, "Does Elijah know?"

That was her response?

It registered with him that she hadn't asked him whether he was joking. Whether he was only saying something ridiculous just to get her off his back about a dating profile.

She hadn't questioned that he had effectively told her that he was gay.

"No." He sighed. "No one does."

"How long?"

He didn't pretend not to know what she was talking about. "We've been together for about three months. We met about a week after I moved here."

He could hear her doing the mental math, practically a shout over the line when she realized he must have already been seeing Dave when she visited him back in March.

Say something.

"Have you always been like this?"

That took him aback. Out of all the things she could have asked next, that hadn't even figured into his list of possibilities.

"Like what, Georgia? Have I always been gay, you mean?"

The profound silence that met his question immediately made him regret firing back at her. She'd probably assumed, like Dave had, that Cam was bi. If Georgia had been depending on Cam's romantic love for LaVerne to provide her with some consolation, he'd just shattered it in a clumsy, thoughtless way.

That wasn't how a good father was supposed to behave.

He forced himself to lower his defenses and was about to apologize when Georgia asked, "Did you ever cheat on Mom?"

It seemed he hadn't done as good a job at lowering his defenses as he'd thought, because the desire to scream at her for questions like that rose too quickly. But he tamped it down hard with the reminder that she was allowed to ask them. No matter what, he and LaVerne had always made sure that they had a strong familial bond. They'd always encouraged the kids to be open and honest, and to expect openness and honesty back.

And of course Georgia would want to know about what mattered to *her*, not to him.

"This is all new to me, Georgia. I mean, acting on my, uh, preferences."

Again, though, she didn't answer right away. He hated these long, charged silences.

Almost a full minute passed before she spoke.

"*Why?*" It sounded like she was about to sob.

"Why what?"

"All of it."

"That will take a very long time to explain." His head felt heavy. "We can talk about it when I'm in Dallas, how about?"

"No." She sounded wild. "I don't want you to come."

What?

"Georgia, I'm not going to miss your graduation. Please calm down. Let's talk tomorrow if that's better, but—"

"Don't tell me to calm down. You *lied* to me. All of us. You— I don't want to talk to you, I don't want to see you. How could you?" The last sentence was a plaintive whisper.

Surely she didn't mean what she was saying. This had gotten out of control way too fast. He never should have been fool enough to lose his temper like that. Over the phone, no less. She was too worked up, and he couldn't be there to see her face or take her hand and tell her he was sorry. To explain.

He gripped the phone tightly, as though it would allow him to hold on to her for a while longer. "Georgia. Listen. Please. I'm sorry. I didn't mean to lie. It was a different time when I married your mother. Even now, the risk it would put us all in back home . . . It *has* to be a secret. I never meant to lie to you, but I *had no choice*."

Choices. Freedom and burden both.

He stopped. Waited for her to respond.

But this time, the silence was different.

"Georgia?"

The dial tone started buzzing in his ear, and he realized Georgia had hung up on him.

He'd been talking, but no one had been listening.

Cam dropped to the floor, feeling suddenly sick.

What had he done?

"Hi, Cam. This is a nice surprise."

Dave sounded happy to hear from Cam in the middle of the day on a Thursday.

It made Cam feel worse than he already did. He'd called Dave immediately after he'd recovered from Georgia hanging up on him, but he was already questioning his decision.

"Hey, Dave. I was, uh, just calling to say hello," he lied, cringing at the stilted way it came out.

"You don't sound too good. Everything okay?"

Of course Dave had realized something was up. Cam fought the urge to lie again. Dave would know, and it would hurt him.

Cam sighed. "Well. Uh, I sort of told Georgia that I'm gay. By accident. And now she doesn't want me at her graduation."

"Whoa." Dave sounded about as stunned as Cam felt. "You— When did that happen?"

"Just now." It felt like someone had punched him in the gut.

"Is she there?"

"No, she called me, and somehow it just came out, and she, uh, didn't take it well. It all happened so fast, I didn't have time to explain before she hung up."

If not for that pain in his stomach, he might even have believed it had never happened, given how quickly—almost comically, if it weren't his whole life in the balance—things had spun out of control.

"Oh, man. Cam. I'm sorry. I—"

But Cam was already talking again, stress coming out him through panicked babbling. "I don't know what to do. I'm not going to *not* be at her graduation. But what kind of memory will it be to sit in the audience and watch her get her diploma while she completely ignores me? I should be angry. I've paid for her education, worked my fingers to the bone to raise her up right. But I can't pretend I didn't hurt her. I—"

"Of course you're going to her graduation." Dave's calm but firm tone stopped the rising hysteria in Cam's mind. "It's a shock to her, that's all. I'm sure she'll come around if you give her a day or two to calm down. She loves you. I know I've never met her, but I can tell simply from the way you talk about her and the stories you tell that you're the most important man in her life."

He wanted to believe it. He'd poured so much into his kids that the possibility of losing their love was—well, it was every fear he'd ever had about revealing his secret, come true.

Cam swallowed hard against the threat of tears.

A clicking noise sounded for a couple of seconds in the background before Dave spoke again, "Do you want some company? I've got a couple more meetings, until two o'clock, but I can come over as soon as they're done."

Cam hesitated, not because he didn't want Dave to come, but because he wanted it too much. He couldn't imagine not having Dave by his side, in good times and bad, for better or worse . . .

Lord save me.

He was in love with Dave Montoya.

"Cam?"

Dave's voice pulled him out of his shock, and Cam shook his head even though he knew Dave couldn't see. "No, I— Thank you. But I actually think I need to go walking for a while. Clear my head."

I love you.

But that love couldn't matter when it came to his *daughter*.

Cam's heart hurt.

After a moment of silence, Dave agreed. "Yeah. Makes sense. Okay, well. I'm here. Call me when you're back home. Maybe tonight?"

"Maybe," Cam murmured.

If Dave came over, he'd *not* push and he'd hold Cam's hand in silence and do all the things that would make Cam fall even more deeply in love with him. He'd make it more difficult for Cam to *choose*.

Dave . . . or his own daughter.

He didn't want this choice.

He could tell Dave was confused by his noncommittal answer, but he couldn't bring himself to deal with it right now. Dave called again that night, but Cam put him off, offering the excuse of being too tired from the emotional day and the three-hour walk.

The next day, Georgia didn't call. Cam's attempts to reach her went straight to voice mail. He'd prayed she'd pick up and they'd resolve this so that he wouldn't have to face—sooner than he'd planned—what he feared would be the end of his happiness.

When Dave phoned again, Cam mumbled an excuse about not wanting to burden him with his problems, and they didn't see one another. On Saturday, he didn't go to the coffee shop. Instead, he stayed in the apartment, sitting at the table and staring out the window, barely able to breathe from the sadness filling his chest.

Shortly before noon, someone knocked on his door. Cam stood up, feeling aches in his muscles from sitting for so long, and trudged to open it. He already knew who it was, though. He knew it was coming and wished like hell he didn't have to go through what was about to happen.

What you're about to do.

The *freedom* of choice was a lie.

He opened the door to find Dave standing in the breezeway, his brow furrowed in concern. "Cam." Dave's eyes were roaming over his face. "Hey. May I come in?"

Cam stepped aside, ushering Dave in but careful not to actually touch him. It would be impossible to get through this if they ended up holding hands or hugging or—or—*anything*, really. Distance was the only solution.

"Are you okay?" Dave made to close the distance between them, but Cam held up a hand, and he watched as a shadow of something angry and scared passed over Dave's face.

"I'm sorry," he croaked. "I needed time to think."

"Do you still need more time?" Dave asked slowly.

Cam swallowed and shook his head.

"I see." Dave had gone rigid. He had to have understood what Cam was about to say.

"Georgia won't take my calls, and she hasn't called me."

"Give her time. I'm sure—"

Lord, help me. Dave's voice had taken on a desperate, pleading tone. Did he feel the same way about Cam that Cam felt for him?

But Cam merely shook his head. It couldn't matter now. He would not lose his child over this.

"I've given her time, and I'm not sure." Even to his own ears, his voice sounded resigned. "I need to fix this."

Dave's jaw was set, and he stared silently at Cam.

Cam was going to have to say the words.

"I can't see you anymore," he whispered. "Because I have to go home right away. I have to put things back the way they were. I'm not going to sell the feed business. I'm going to Georgia's graduation, and I'm going to get her forgiveness, and then I'm driving straight to Bitter."

"And that's it? You won't be back?"

Cam nodded. It was the choice he'd made, but for some reason, instead of making him feel better, his body seemed to be crumbling in on itself now that he'd spoken the words aloud.

Dave crossed his arms over his chest. "You're ending this because one person doesn't approve?"

"She's not just one person," Cam protested. "This is my *daughter*. Losing my family and everything I held dear was what kept me away from this—" he gestured between himself and Dave "—in the first place."

"What is *this*?" Dave demanded.

"It—it's love." Cam could barely get the words out, but he *needed* to.

Dave glared at him for a long time before finally curling his lip in disgust and practically spitting out, "This isn't love." And then he turned and walked to the door, grabbed at the handle, and wrenched it open.

"Dave!" Cam cried.

But Dave didn't wait. He strode over the threshold, and yanked the door shut behind him with a loud slam.

Cam raced to the door and pulled it open again, but from the parking lot the sound of a car engine starting up told him he was already too late. Dave had moved too fast.

"We can take things slow."

Cam nearly sobbed at the memory.

It dawned on him that, for all his talk about being in Austin only temporarily, he'd been preparing himself to stay here.

With Dave.

He ran down the stairs, bare feet stinging on the concrete, not even sure what he was trying to accomplish.

When he hit the sidewalk in front of the building, Dave had already driven halfway across the parking lot.

Gone.

Cam stood there, the reality of what he'd just done hitting him full force.

He should have known that his chance at happiness was destined to lead to heartbreak.

Dejected, he turned back around and trudged upstairs to his apartment.

Time to pack it in, put it all away. That was his lot in life, and the only way to save his relationship with Georgia.

2015

"Cam, are you busy?" LaVerne's voice registered weakly from the living room.

He was taking down the light fixture in the kitchen, standing on a stepstool with a screwdriver as he tried to remove the glass casing without dropping it. It was mid-August and hot in their small, no-air-conditioning house, and his hands were slippery with sweat. "A little bit," he called back. "Whatcha need?"

He heard the approach of her wheelchair. "I think I have to go to the hospital." Her voice sounded off. Really off.

He whipped his head down to the doorway that connected the living room to the kitchen and gasped at the sight of LaVerne sitting there, her face a dull gray-yellow instead of a rich brown. Her mouth was oddly slack and her body was shaking—

Crash!

The glass casing shattered on the tiled floor, making Cam jump with surprise.

LaVerne barely reacted.

No. No, not yet.

He jumped off the stool, throwing the screwdriver to the floor, and rushed to her side, grabbing her hand. "What's wrong? What are you feeling?"

"Bad," was all she got out, before her eyes rolled back in her head and she fainted.

Oh, man. Cam could feel panic threatening.

Stay calm. Call 911.

Not quite an hour later, the gurney that the paramedics had put her on was being wheeled into the emergency room of the regional hospital. They'd revived her in the ambulance during the long ride, but she was still too weak to speak.

They immediately hooked her up to a myriad of machines and needles, a team of medical professionals swarming around her bed as they poked and prodded and tried to diagnose the *bad*.

Cam was sent into the waiting room, where he paced for a while before Georgia, who had followed in the truck, showed up. Thank God it was summer break from school and she'd been home for a couple of months, hanging out at a nearby friend's house when LaVerne had fainted. He'd called Georgia to come home while he was waiting for the ambulance to show up, and she'd arrived at the house at the same time as the paramedics.

"Any news?" Georgia was breathless. She must have run inside from the parking lot.

"Nothing yet."

She fell against him, shaking and crying. He stroked her hair and patted her back.

My poor little girl.

He prayed LaVerne wouldn't pass away before Georgia got to say good-bye. Elijah was deployed in the Middle East, and it was impossible to get ahold of him right away, but he'd bear the news much better than Georgia, anyway. She'd always been the more sensitive of the two.

After a little while, Georgia calmed down, and they were just about to sit when Dr. Phillips approached.

Cam turned to him and shook his hand. "How is she?"

Dr. Phillips frowned. "Stable. But I'm afraid her kidneys are in poor shape."

Georgia whimpered.

"What does it mean for— What's the prognosis?" Cam asked.

"I'm going to put her on the donor list." Dr. Phillips gave a small shrug. "However, given her preexisting condition, I don't have high hopes for a transplant."

Georgia gripped Cam's arm tightly.

Cam nodded. "I understand. What do you think, then? How much longer?"

Dr. Phillips looked at Georgia, then back at Cam, seemingly hesitant to share an opinion in front of her, but then finally he gave a frank appraisal. "A few more months. Six, tops."

Six months at the most.

Elijah would be allowed to come home at Christmas for two weeks. Cam prayed she could hold on until then.

Dr. Phillips excused himself, and Georgia began crying in earnest. "What are we going to do, Daddy?"

He closed his eyes against the rush of pain. She was twenty years old but still called him *Daddy* when she was hurt or scared. It was Georgia he was worried about now. He had accepted years ago that LaVerne wouldn't be around much longer, but the suffering of his children was still almost too painful to bear. Once LaVerne was gone, his children would be all he had left.

He held on tightly to Georgia and let her cry until she was too exhausted to cry any more.

Chapter Seventeen

On Sunday evening, Cam was packing up his things in the apartment when his phone rang, and for the short span of time between the first trill and when he saw the screen, he allowed himself to hope that it was Dave.

It wasn't.

"Hey, Elijah." Cam forced himself to smile, if only to keep Elijah from hearing his despondence.

"Dad. What's going on? I just hung up with Georgia, and she was really upset. We were talking about her graduation plans, and she said you two had a fight and I should call you."

Cam felt a sharp stab of fear. It was happening. His secret was out and it was getting spread around, putting him in harm's way, risking everything he loved.

Calm down. This is your son you're talking to.

"What did she tell you about what happened?"

Elijah huffed. "Nothing. She just said she'd told you not to come to her graduation, but she regrets that, but she still doesn't want to talk to you. She asked me to call you and tell you that you should come."

Some of the tightness Cam had been carrying around since Thursday eased.

"I told her she sounded like a spoiled brat and she should call you herself, but she wouldn't listen." Elijah made a sound of disapproval. "Why didn't you tell her she can pay you back all that money you spent to put her through school if she's going to act like that?"

Cam had thought about it, but he'd shocked Georgia pretty badly. He'd neither the motivation nor the desire, really, to add another issue on top of their already fractured relationship. He never thought he'd reach a point where he hoped to feel close enough again to his daughter to berate her over her disrespect.

In the meantime, he could and would do better with Elijah.

"Elijah . . . with Georgia, I . . . We were talking about something, and I lost my temper."

Elijah snorted. "She makes me lose my temper all the time."

"Not quite like this. I said something—" Cam stopped and took a deep breath. "I've been keeping something from the two of you for a long time. I want to say that first. It's a pretty big thing."

"Did you cheat on Mom?" Elijah was immediately on the offensive.

"Lord, no. Why do the two of you both assume such a thing?" Cam frowned. He didn't think he was the kind of guy who made people think he'd have an affair.

"Georgia asked that too? Why would she— *Oh.*"

Elijah went suddenly, deathly silent.

That had sounded like a realization.

"Elijah." Cam strove for calm. "I love you and Georgia more than anything in this world. I want you to—I *need* you to know that."

"I know." Elijah sounded hoarse. "I— Dad, I *know*. All of it. But I need you to . . . just say it."

Oh. Lord.

He wished he didn't have to say the words to someone whose opinion mattered so much. Yes, Georgia knew, but it had all come about so suddenly that he hadn't taken the time to fully consider what her reaction would be before he'd told her.

Losing Georgia's support was tearing him apart, and if Elijah abandoned him, too . . .

It would be unbearable.

Still, he had to honor his son's demand to know. Elijah's request mattered too.

He took a deep breath and on the exhale . . .

"I'm gay."

It came out trembling, almost a question, but he'd said it clearly enough. He was surprised, in fact. He'd never had a sit-down confession like this, intentionally sharing his biggest secret with someone who shouldn't have known.

And yet, somehow it was much easier than he'd expected it to be. Except for the silence coming from Elijah's end.

Please don't turn me away. Please don't cut me out of your life.

"It would have been better in person. I hadn't meant for you to find out this way," Cam rushed to explain, trying to keep Elijah on the line. And Elijah hadn't hung up on him yet. That was worth something.

Too much time passed, though, and Cam was about to try again, just to fill the silence, when Elijah spoke.

"Did you ever? Expect me to find out, I mean. Were you ever going to tell us?"

Surprisingly, though, Elijah didn't sound accusatory. Just . . . *curious*.

It calmed Cam somewhat. At least, enough to answer honestly.

"No. I hadn't intended to tell anyone, ever."

Elijah sucked in a breath so sharply that Cam heard it crackle over the line.

"Ever?"

Knowing what he knew now, Cam agreed with the sense of disbelief coming from his son. Had he really thought he could live out his days with such a secret?

Possibly. He'd already done it for fifty years. What was another few decades?

But he couldn't deny how depressing that sounded.

"That had been the plan," Cam admitted.

"What changed? Why did you tell Georgia, even if it was by accident?"

Cam scrubbed a hand over his face and blinked, focusing on the wall in front of him as he answered. "I met someone. Georgia was pushing me to get a dating profile and wouldn't take no for an answer. Letting her continue to push me felt like cheating on him." Cam huffed out a laugh. "Ironic."

"Yeah." Elijah laughed too, but it was short and tense sounding. There was a moment of silence before Elijah gave a little cough. "So."

"So." Cam braced himself for rejection.

"Listen, Dad . . . I, uh, I think I need a little time to kind of, uh, think about this. If that's okay."

Cam's heart squeezed. He'd known it was coming, but it still hurt so much. "Yeah. Maybe we can at least talk on Friday before—"

"Hey, Dad," Elijah broke in. "I mean, I just need to get off the phone and chill for a bit, like, right now. I'm still meeting up with you in Dallas for the graduation. I should be able to get there by Friday afternoon. Tim will handle the store until Sunday. We'll probably talk before then, anyway."

The grip on Cam's heart eased. "That sounds good. Thank you, Elijah. You have no idea—"

"What's this guy's name, anyway? The one you care about so much that even the mention of a dating profile felt like cheating?"

Beneath the interrogatory approach, Cam could hear light teasing, and he was glad Elijah didn't seem to be shutting him out, but the reminder of Dave had the pain returning, sharp and debilitating.

"We broke up," he practically wheezed. "I'm going back to Bitter after the graduation."

There was a long pause, but finally Elijah spoke again. "We'll talk more soon. If not before Friday, then drive safe, Dad." He paused, and before Cam could return the sentiment, Elijah added, "I love you."

His heart squeezed so tight it was painful. "I love you too, son," Cam whispered.

And then there was a click, and the line went dead.

On Thursday, Cam packed up his truck, cleaned the apartment, and dropped the keys at the management office.

He'd told himself not to look back as he left, but he couldn't stop looking in the rearview as he merged onto the toll road heading north. After a while, he realized he was being a fool. What was he thinking, that Dave would come driving up behind him at ninety miles an hour and say . . .

What? It was Cam's fault. Cam's problem. Dave had been right to walk away without looking back.

Cam arrived into Dallas in the early afternoon and headed directly to the hotel to check in. He was rumpled and sore from the long drive and feeling more than a little emotionally wrung out too.

When he walked into the lobby, though, the sight that greeted him had his pulse perking up, his heart jumping with sudden, blinding hope.

"Georgia."

He stopped short of the low patterned couch in the lounge where his daughter was sitting, wearing an expression that looked a lot like the one she had on her face any time she'd got into trouble as a kid.

Ashamed. Sad.

She stood up slowly, still eyeing him warily, as though he'd reject her right here in the lobby of the Holiday Inn.

But she didn't move otherwise, and after a moment of stunned immobility, he was the one to rush forward. "Sweetheart, what are you doing here?"

Her face crumpled, and she pitched forward, falling into him in a way so reminiscent of the night LaVerne was taken to the hospital that he nearly broke down in tears too.

"Daddy. I'm so sorry. So, so sorry. I was shocked, and I didn't handle it the way— I mean, I thought I'd be fine with you dating—I was the one trying to get you to date, even. I *know*. I know it was stupid to be so upset about you seeing someone new, and on top of that you were telling me that you're . . . *gay* . . . and it felt like you were *completely* abandoning her. All I could think about was how much I missed Mom, and no matter who you were dating, it wasn't right that you were moving on and leaving her behind and leaving *us* behind and—" She stopped to suck in a deep breath, but he held up a hand before she could start talking again.

"It's okay. I know it was a shock. I shouldn't have lost my temper, and I'm sorry too."

He felt her relax against him. "Elijah called me and said I was a spoiled brat. He told me I didn't deserve to have *anyone* at my graduation. Can you believe that?" Her voice was muffled against his shirt.

He couldn't help but laugh at that. *Man*, they were both so young.

She pulled back and looked up at him, eyes wide and shining with tears. "I want you to know that I'm not, you know, mad or anything. About you being gay. I know we still need to talk more." She let out a small huff of amusement. "A *lot* more. But Elijah also said you'd ended things with your . . . the guy, and I thought talking about that might be a good place to start."

She looked away again when she said the last part, though. He wasn't sure it was because she actually found it distasteful and was trying to put on a good face for his sake, or that she was still embarrassed over raising such a ruckus about it in the first place. Either way, it seemed it was all still too raw to push the issue.

Dave would have done that. Stepped back. Not pushed.

He didn't want to think about Dave.

Cam felt himself shrinking away. Shutting down. He set his jaw and shook his head. "I don't want to talk about that, Georgia." Some things had to be hard lines. "It's over, and I'm heading back to Bitter on Sunday." He forced a smile. "It would be great if you came to stay there before you start work, if you want. We haven't talked about what you're going to do before your lease starts."

Georgia would start her job in a couple of weeks at one of the Dallas news stations, working as a junior producer, but she couldn't move in to her apartment until the first of June.

She stared at him, frowning. "Dad. You were happy. When I saw you back in March, you—"

Pushing.

"I said I don't want to talk about it." He didn't quite snap at her, but she drew back, clearly cowed by his tone. He made himself relax and offer at least a conciliatory smile. He couldn't risk things blowing up again. "Why don't I check in, and then we can go for a walk? Maybe have some coffee?"

He didn't want to fight any more. For at least a few hours, he needed to pretend that everything was okay.

But by the time he got through the weekend—Elijah's arrival, the barrage of questions, the toll of having to dig deep inside himself to explain all the choices he'd made in his life, and finally the actual graduation ceremony in which he clapped and cheered and worked like a dog to keep the hollow, hurting part of himself locked away—a few hours had turned into a few days, and he was on the edge of despair.

Who would have thought that he could get his heart broken for the first time at fifty-five?

Dave didn't break your heart. You did that to yourself.

Now he was going back to a life he wasn't even sure he wanted anymore, but that he had chosen out of fear.

Just like the first time around.

He turned up the volume on the radio in his truck as he sped down the highway on Sunday en route to Bitter, trying to drown out the sound of his keening emptiness. By the time he pulled into the driveway of the house where he'd lived for thirty-five years, but now seemed strangely unfamiliar, he was exhausted.

Still, he found the energy to walk inside, make up his bed that hadn't been slept in for months, cook a small meal, and greet Elijah and Georgia when they, too, arrived from Dallas, having driven in separate cars.

It was only when he slipped between his sheets that night, in the dark quiet of familiar strangeness, that he allowed the exhaustion to flow out of his body as he wept for everything he'd lost.

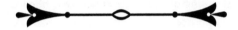

2016

LaVerne's eyes were closed.

Cam reached out and felt her wrist, a habit he'd developed over the past few days. There was still a pulse. Weak, but it was there.

His shoulders relaxed. He hadn't even realized he'd been holding them up near his ears.

He'd brought her to this place five days ago. She'd waited until after Christmas, after all. They'd spent the holiday together, and LaVerne had insisted on going to the airport to see Elijah off on his flight back to the Middle East, where he'd serve the last few months of his military career.

In the car on the way back home, she'd talked about the night of her graduation, how that had been the night Cam's father had died, but Cam had known what LaVerne was really saying.

They'd all known.

Two days later, Dr. Phillips had admitted her into hospice. Her kidneys had completely shut down, he'd said, and it was down to a matter of days. Georgia was still in town. They'd spent almost every waking hour by LaVerne's side, talking together until she could no longer speak, but even then Cam had kept the conversation going for Georgia's sake.

Georgia had gone home a few hours ago to get some sleep, and Cam had fallen silent, dozing on and off until he'd woken up with a start at quarter past three in the morning.

The witching hour.

He gently lowered LaVerne's hands back to the bed after taking her pulse and then simply sat there, blinking unsteadily, for the next ten minutes.

That was when he heard it.

"Cam?" LaVerne's voice was barely audible from the fluffy pillows she lay against, but it still sounded like a shot fired in the otherwise silent room.

"LaVerne?" He immediately scrambled closer to her, leaning over the metal railing of the medical bed that filled up most of the room. It was supposed to feel like a home, to make the patients more comfortable, but the end result simply felt like a slightly less fluorescent hospital room. With more lace.

"Cam," she whispered again.

He could feel her hand moving against the sheets, almost as though it was searching for something, and he reached down to take her fingers gently in his. "What is it?"

The movement stopped, and he realized it was his hand she'd been searching for.

She looked up at him and smiled, her face appearing so unexpectedly youthful that it took him a moment to understand why.

She was no longer in pain.

"I love you."

The words sounded much clearer than her earlier whisper.

And he knew. They both *knew*.

"I love you too, LaVerne." Maybe not the way a lover would have, or the way a husband should have, but he loved her deeply, just the same.

And it was the best way he could think of to say good-bye.

Her smile broadened, and her fingers squeezed tightly around his, strength flowing out of her.

Out of her. Draining. Leaving.

"*LaVerne*," he said, but there was no answer as, in the medical bed in that not-quite-home hospice room, LaVerne released her last breath.

And then . . . there was only silence.

Chapter Eighteen

Cam dragged his suitcase into his bedroom from where it had been sitting, untouched, in the hallway for the past week.

They'd all gone to church that morning, and now Elijah and Georgia were visiting their cousin Theo and his family while Cam begged off, saying he needed to go home and rest for a while.

It was mostly true, anyway. His nerves needed a break. He felt jumpy and angry and depressed in equal and constant turns. The kids had noticed. Georgia had apologized every few hours, and it finally made him snap at her.

"Stop apologizing! I don't want to hear it!"

It was making him regret too much. So he'd shouted. Roared, really. But she hadn't backed down. Instead, she'd told him to go apologize to Dave, hoping that the same humility she was exercising would save Cam too.

He wished it were that easy.

For his part, Elijah had suggested that Cam sell the store, after all, but Cam had refused. What reason would he have to get up every day if even that was gone?

Come now, you're being melodramatic.

He sighed and rolled his eyes at himself. True, he wasn't *that* down. But he'd never felt this out of sorts before, and he didn't like it.

He set the suitcase atop the bureau and unzipped it, pulling out clothes and sorting them into the drawers. A couple of pictures in frames came next, which he set aside to deal with later. He grabbed a folded towel, starting to walk it to the bathroom to stow in the small linen closet, when something fell out of it and clattered to the floor. Another frame. It was lying facedown, and he hoped the glass hadn't shattered. He didn't need the aggravation right now.

He bent and scooped it up, relieved to see no glass pieces on the floor. He turned it over to see which photo it was . . .

And stilled.

Choices.

Not a photo, after all. The sight of the framed embroidery felt so much like a punch to the gut that he actually let out a hard *whoosh* of air, curling forward as he clutched the frame to his chest.

He'd been wrong. So wrong. Walking away from Dave at the first sign of trouble had been a terrible choice, and his kids had seen it before he had.

Youth. They were more accustomed to having choices and making concrete decisions out of so many nebulous possibilities. It made them wiser than he was. He should have seen it.

Should have. Could have . . .

But what was he going to do about it now?

Maybe . . . maybe it *was* that easy.

He stood there for not even a minute longer before springing into action, leaving the open suitcase behind as he raced through the house, grabbing up wallet, keys, and phone. He shoved his feet into his boots and clopped out into the heat and over to his truck.

He'd just opened the driver's-side door when Elijah and Georgia pulled into the driveway, returning from their visit. He watched impatiently as they got out. He'd give them a quick greeting, then say good-bye and be off.

"Hey, Dad. Where you going?" Elijah was still in his church clothes, and it struck Cam how much of a man his son had become.

"I have to go to Austin. Just for a short time. I'll probably be back tonight." Cam watched as Georgia came around the front of Elijah's car, eyes widening at Cam's declaration.

"It's almost a five-hour drive one way. You won't even get there until after seven o'clock. It won't be safe to drive home tonight, especially after . . ."

They all knew what he was getting at.

If Cam was coming home tonight, it would be because Dave had rejected his plea for forgiveness. Cam might be too emotional, too upset, too . . . whatever. Driving wasn't a great idea.

"Then I'll stay the night and be back early, in time to open up the store," Cam told them.

Georgia shook her head. "No, Dad."

He opened his mouth to give her a piece of his mind, to tell her to stop standing in the way of his happiness, but before he could say a word, she added, "I'm coming with you."

What?

Elijah nodded in agreement. "Me too. Tim can open up tomorrow. I'll give him a call. But we're *both* coming with. It's time for us to be there for you, Dad. Past time."

Cam's heart was so full, it felt ready to burst. He stepped forward and wrapped an arm around each kid, pulling them close.

Half an hour later, they were on the road, heading toward an uncertain future, and yet Cam had never before felt so sure of anything in his life.

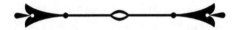

Elijah whistled when they pulled into Dave's driveway. "This is his house?"

"Yeah." Cam probably sounded too wistful, but he had fond memories of things that had happened in this house. He stopped the truck in front of the garage. "Man, I hope he's home."

"Well, let's go and find out," Georgia said from the back. "I gotta get out and stretch my legs, anyway."

Oh, man. Cam hadn't thought about what would actually happen when they got here. In his mind, his kids hadn't been a part of his apology to Dave. But if Dave forgave him, and actually decided to take him back, Elijah and Georgia would have to be a part of that life. Perhaps it was good to begin—again—as he meant to go on.

Cam got out of the truck, Elijah and Georgia hopping out on the other side. They followed him to the front door, where he rang the bell before he could chicken out.

They waited.

And waited.

After a minute, Cam realized that Dave wasn't going to answer the door. He probably wasn't home.

He turned around to Elijah and Georgia, shaking his head. "I'll have to come back another time. I don't think—"

But just then, he heard the lock turning, and he whipped back around to see—

"Jacqui?"

Dave's sister stood in the doorway, glaring at Cam.

"You'd better have come to apologize."

"He did," Georgia fired back, and he could feel her step close to him, just behind his left shoulder.

Jacqui's eyes cut to Georgia as though she'd just realized that Cam wasn't alone, and her expression immediately turned contrite. "I—"

"I did come to apologize," Cam cut her off. "I came to beg. And I was going to come alone, but the kids insisted on tagging along."

A small smile tipped the corners of Jacqui's mouth, and Cam could tell she was trying to fight back a full grin.

Georgia must have seen it too, because she pressed the advantage. "Dad's been moping around for days. I've never seen him like this, and since it was all my fault to begin with, I'm here to apologize too."

Cam held up a hand. "Georgia. Could you please let me handle this? At least let me go first."

Jacqui laughed then, unable to hold it back any longer, but sobered quickly. "Dave's been really down too. You hurt him bad, Cam."

"I know." He said it with strength of conviction, not shying away from the mistake he'd made.

Jacqui stared at him for a bit before finally opening the door wide with a sigh. "Come on in, then. I'll go get him."

"I'm right here."

Cam heard the voice behind the door a second before Dave stepped into view.

Lord. The man looked *rough*. Dark circles ringed his eyes, and his face was gaunt, stubble hiding his cheeks and jaw. He was dressed in jeans and what appeared to be a clean shirt, at least, but given his appearance otherwise, the clothes were probably Jacqui's doing.

"*Dave,*" Cam whispered.

He heard Georgia gasp, but luckily she didn't say anything, and Cam watched as Dave's gaze flicked from Georgia to Elijah, then settled on Cam. Dave nodded in acknowledgment, probably out of respect for the kids, but there was anger in his eyes. Pain.

Not great, but at least there was *feeling*. Cam could work with that.

"I'm sorry. Dave, I'm so sorry," he blurted. It wasn't how he'd meant to say it, but now that he was here, all he could think of was simple honesty.

Dave wasn't walking away or shutting the door on him, either, so Cam continued.

"I shouldn't have cut you out of my life. It was . . . I was running away, and I see that now. I used my fight with Georgia as an excuse, but the truth was that it was my own problem that I was so afraid. I couldn't see the choices in front of me because I was blinded by fear. The way I grew up . . . Well, I got so used to that way of thinking, believing I only had a choice of good or bad, one or the other, with nothing in between, that I couldn't keep myself from falling into that pattern again. I hurt you. I hurt myself. And I miss you so desperately . . ."

Cam was having a harder time speaking with every word. He was on the verge of tears, but he pushed through, needing to say one more thing.

"Because I do love you. I've fallen in love with you, and even if you don't forgive me, even if I never get to kiss you again, I want you to know that you were the one who gifted me with something I've never had before: a choice to live the way I was meant to live. To love the way I was meant to love."

Tears were dripping down his face now. He'd never felt so raw and vulnerable before, but he couldn't make himself care. He blinked away the sheen that blurred his vision, unwilling to look away from Dave's face.

He was staring at Cam and frowning.

No one said a word. It was as though time had stopped on a single collectively held breath.

Dave started to shake his head.

No. It hurt. It hurt so much.

Cam braced himself for the rejection.

But Dave didn't say anything. Instead, he stepped forward, bringing his hands to Cam's cheeks, drawing their lips together.

"Oh my gosh, it's so *sweet*."

Cam vaguely registered Georgia's weepy-sounding voice as he wrapped his arms around Dave's back, holding him tightly in a warm, relieved embrace. Dave's lips were soft against his, and the kiss was relatively chaste, most likely in deference to their audience, but it still communicated everything Cam needed to know.

I forgive you.

That was Dave's choice, and Cam was grateful for it. For all the pain, all the risk, and all the love.

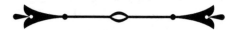

Later that night, Cam lay in Dave's bed, his hand on Dave's chest. The kids were staying with Jacqui for the night and would return in the morning to go back to Bitter.

Cam would go back too. Long enough to make arrangements for selling the store and the house. Breaking the ties that had both kept him going and held him back for so long.

He was just on the edge of sleep when he heard it, a barely audible whisper from the soft pillow next to him.

"Cam?" Dave's voice was deep and gentle.

"Yeah?"

"I love you."

Cam picked up his head and found Dave's eyes in the moonlight. "I love you too."

TELL THE WORLD THIS BOOK WAS

GOOD | BAD | SO-SO

Dear Reader,

Thank you for reading Audra North's *Midlife Crisis*!

We know your time is precious and you have many, many entertainment options, so it means a lot that you've chosen to spend your time reading. We really hope you enjoyed it.

We'd be honored if you'd consider posting a review—good or bad—on sites like **Amazon, Barnes & Noble, Kobo, Goodreads, Twitter, Facebook, Tumblr,** and your blog or website. We'd also be honored if you told your friends and family about this book. Word of mouth is a book's lifeblood!

For more information on upcoming releases, author interviews, blog tours, contests, giveaways, and more, please sign up for our weekly, spam-free newsletter and visit us around the web:

Newsletter: tinyurl.com/RiptideSignup
Twitter: twitter.com/RiptideBooks
Facebook: facebook.com/RiptidePublishing
Goodreads: tinyurl.com/RiptideOnGoodreads
Tumblr: riptidepublishing.tumblr.com

Thank you so much for Reading the Rainbow!

RiptidePublishing.com

Acknowledgments

I am forever indebted to my husband and children for being the best support system I could wish for. Without their willingness to give me a room of my own, I would never have been able to write this book.

Thank you to my editor, Sarah Lyons, who took this raw story and made it so much better with her wisdom, insight, and precision, all while allowing me the space to maintain my own voice. Sarah, editors like you are hard to come by, and I really appreciate your many talents.

Finally, I want to thank my agent, Courtney Miller-Callihan, for making this book happen in the first place. It started with a Facebook post and turned into a novel!

ALSO BY

Audra North

ABOUT
the Author

Audra North is a contemporary romance author of more than twenty romances, including the Stanton Family series, the Hard Driving series, and the Pushing the Boundaries series. She is the owner and publisher of Pink Kayak Press, which focuses on the publication of diverse romance works. *Winter Rain*, a Pink Kayak Press anthology, won a gold medal in the 2015 Independent Publisher Awards.

Audra enjoys speaking to writing groups and at industry conferences. She is also an avid jogger and loves running marathons. She has three children and lives with her family outside of Boston.

For more about Audra, and to sign up for her newsletter, visit audranorth.com.

Connect with Audra:
Website: audranorth.com
Twitter: @AudraNorth
Facebook: AudraNorthAuthor

Enjoy more stories like
Midlife Crisis
at RiptidePublishing.com!

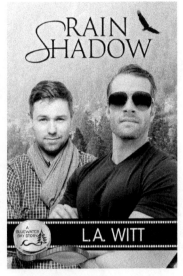

Spun!
ISBN: 978-1-62649-589-0

Rain Shadow
ISBN: 978-1-62649-367-4

Earn Bonus Bucks!
Earn 1 Bonus Buck for each dollar you spend. Find out how at
RiptidePublishing.com/news/bonus-bucks.

Win Free Ebooks for a Year!
Pre-order coming soon titles directly through our site and you'll
receive one entry into a drawing for a chance to win free books for
a year! Get the details at RiptidePublishing.com/contests.

CPSIA information can be obtained
at www.ICGtesting.com
Printed in the USA
FSHW04n1334120418
46905FS